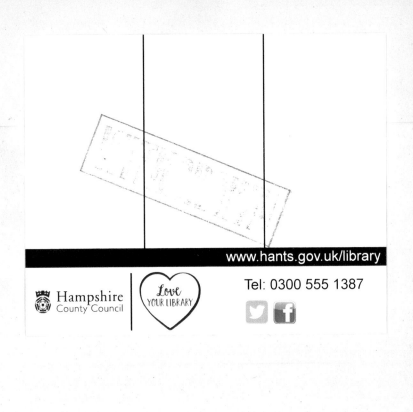

www.hants.gov.uk/library

Tel: 0300 555 1387

Hampshire
County Council

Love
YOUR LIBRARY

D0756119

C016478529

KAREN McLEOD

In Search of the Missing Eyelash

VINTAGE BOOKS
London

Published by Vintage 2008

10 9

Copyright © Karen Mcleod 2007

The author is grateful for permission to reprint lines from the following:
'(They Long To Be) Close To You' Words by Hal David & Music by
Burt Bacharach © Copyright 1963 Casa Music Incorporated/New
Hidden Valley Music Company, USA. Universal/MCA Music Limited
(50%). Used by permission of Music Sales Limited and P&P Songs. All
Rights Reserved. International Copyright Secured. *On Photography* by
Susan Sontag (Allen Lane, 1978) Copyright © Susan Sontag,
1973, 1974, 1977.

Karen Mcleod has asserted her right under the Copyright, Designs
and Patents Act 1988 to be identified as the author of this work

This book is sold subject to the condition that it shall not,
by way of trade or otherwise, be lent, resold, hired out,
or otherwise circulated without the publisher's prior
consent in any form of binding or cover other than that
in which it is published and without a similar condition,
including this condition, being imposed on the
subsequent purchaser

First published in Great Britain by Jonathan Cape in 2007

Vintage
Random House, 20 Vauxhall Bridge Road,
London SW1V 2SA

www.vintage-books.co.uk

Addresses for companies within The Random House Group Limited
can be found at: www.randomhouse.co.uk/offices.htm

The Random House Group Limited Reg. No. 954009

A CIP catalogue record for this book
is available from the British Library

ISBN 9780099507970

Penguin Random House is committed to a sustainable future for
our business, our readers and our planet. This book is made from
Forest Stewardship Council® certified paper.

Printed and bound in Great Britain by Clays Ltd, Elcograf S.p.A.

To all the girls I've loved before

In Search of the Missing Eyelash

Why do birds suddenly appear
Every time you are near?
Just like me, they long to be
Close to you.

Why do stars fall down from the sky
Every time you walk by?
Just like me, they long to be
Close to you.

Burt Bacharach and Hal David,
'Close to You'

Through photos, each family constructs a portrait-chronicle of itself, a portable kit of images that bears witness to its connectedness. It hardly matters what activities are photographed as long as photos get taken and are cherished.

Susan Sontag, *On Photography*

1

I woke up in a foreign armpit.

Her arm is a pale orange from the street light outside, and as I lift up my head, her arm stays there, unmoved across the bed. From what I can see there is a few days' stubble in her armpit, as her breast has rolled sideways off her chest almost covering it up. Her chest doesn't appear to be going up or down. But in the same moment it takes me to recall her wetting herself at the end of my road last night, she's opened up her mouth and a gentle snore reveals that she isn't dead at all.

My tongue is dry and my teeth are all furred up. I roll out of bed onto the floor and find my clothes there in a pile. I realise from the air that I am naked. Her bra is on top of my clothes; it is large with two smiling wires under the bulletproof-like silvery cups. I remember she'd put her wet trousers in my bath, and I was drunk but very accommodating, as I had given her my only flannel to have a wash. I crawl to the door and then along the corridor and I can still feel the alcohol in my veins. I feel like laughing as I don't recognise myself. I am a naughty bachelor in a bad American film who, in the rude glare of the fridge light, might drink juice out of a carton messily in his socks and baggy underpants. A rock song will come on and I will have ruffled hair and a look around my lips like I have just done it, and because I have a strange girl in my bed, will move my head up and down to the wild guitar playing, knowing I had been fucking great.

But film studs need an audience and I would have to wait until morning to tell Petula downstairs.

When I find and flick on the light switch, I am pleased to find it is my kitchen. I haven't lived here long enough to know the flat as if it is my outer body; the house I lived in before, the house we grew up in, is still where I think I live when I am half asleep. It's the place I dream about. I turn the light off and look at the night, set like a jelly outside the window. It's that lovely hour when I can believe that the sun will never appear and maybe time has stopped, and there is no pressure to think or not think about her or to find Simon.

You remember? Yes. Si, as I called him, is/was my brother and I'll tell you about her later.

So I shiver on the lino and open the fridge door and look for the juice from the stud film and find a familiar comfort in how my fridge door opens and how the light comes on. It makes me feel real. I can see parts of myself lit up. In the house I used to stay in with her, the bulb had gone in the fridge and it was wrong opening the fridge to no light (a lot of things stopped working around that time, I got blamed for the sandwich toaster and door-bell).

Among the crumbs on the empty glass shelves there is a carton of fresh grapefruit juice, out of date by a few weeks. When I first moved in I'd bought it as a cocktail mixer. I close the fridge door, and fill two glasses with water from the tap, one for me and one for the stranger. Through the window above the sink I can see that everyone is asleep in the houses opposite, their curtains pulled tightly together holding in their lives.

I go back into the bedroom and get slowly into bed. She isn't snoring and has turned over. I can see her back, her hair is long and it has stretched across to touch my pillow. I hold my breath as I don't know what else to do, but I want to warm my feet on her. I'm not sure how we had got from dancing near one another to her coming home with me last night. I think I might have winked a few times. I never thought winking worked but it's easier than speaking, especially if you've practised in the mirror.

And here she is in my bed, proof that winking works and I'm not too pear-shaped, as she had called me just before the whole lasagne affair unfurled. I'd met someone else and out of all the girls in the club the stranger had picked me.

My eyes have now adjusted to the light and I lift up the duvet to examine the stranger's body. She has a swimmer's figure as far as I can tell from her back, which is hunched away from me, broad shoulders and dark wavy hair. Her bottom isn't full like mine, it is a bit like a man's and very pale, almost blotchy in the light. I decide not to close my eyes for the rest of the night, because that would make the morning come and she would wake up and be who she is and not who I can make her into, for now.

I think about touching myself but I suppose it might be disrespectful, like masturbating with a dead person next to you. So, I lift up the duvet again and look down and am shocked to see that my hip bone has disappeared. I press where it used to jut out and can feel the buried bone underneath a layer of fat. My legs are like sausages near to bursting in a dimpled skin that is too tight. I brush my hands over my soft stomach and squeeze two handfuls of flesh and then find another around the base of my ribs and push the two rolls together and I find I can create different folds and a face with the line which marks my belly button. I turn on my side and feel my belly spill onto the mattress in front. I can't remember how I'd got so fat or when it started or when I wasn't. But I have no long mirrors in the flat; the ones I have all cut me off from the neck down. I put my hand back onto my thigh and then go to touch the stranger's back, but stop myself. Instead, I close my eyes and with my hand rubbing between my legs make the stranger her for the brief while it takes to lead me to gasp and feel my head pop with the feeling that heats up my toes.

I'll confess to you now that I have fancied garlic bread for three months, uncontrollably and often late at night, which is unusual for spring when we are told we naturally want to take a good look at ourselves and say no to seconds. My body is still set on padding itself out like it does in early winter.

Lately, when I know it's my bedtime, I have taken to raiding the freezer, banging in the ready-to-bake garlic baguettes pumped with garlic butter and, because I can't wait, removing them when they are still pale-looking, not able to wait for it to drip down my face, dipping my tongue into the semi-frozen centre of the bread. It used to be jam-filled doughnuts, pinged ready in the microwave in seconds, and I am worried that I am leaning towards phallic-shaped food, in case it is a secret desire to sleep with some man which I haven't yet realised. But that would make me as bad as her, wouldn't it?

I have noticed flesh has grown under my arms and my thighs gently rub together when I walk down the street. I haven't looked at myself for weeks, which means I go out not knowing what I look like. It's easy if you don't have a long mirror. I still study my face in the one in the bathroom and I don't think it has got that much bigger, but then again you see you those large ladies with their faces still pretty and perfectly formed on top of their big bodies, don't you?

And yet there is a woman in my bed, who out of all the other women in the club liked me and came home with me. Except I'm not sure if anything happened and I can hardly ask her in case it was amazing sex and I'm her best yet and she has already fallen in love with me. I don't want to spoil what might be, in her mind, a perfect night, so I won't ask.

My life is different. In one night it has changed and moved a little, maybe not that far forwards but certainly not backwards, to how it's been, which I'm always afraid of. It's just like the night when Petula met her secret boyfriend, Ewan, and she said the predictability of the next day vanished. She'd said people on the train had stared at her as if there was something different about her . . . as if her skin was telling them her secrets.

2

Si, as I often called him, is/was my brother.

But then you know that, don't you?

In the photo I have of him he is holding a snooker cue and grinning from ear to ear. His jumper is a little too small for him and his friend Colin, who is black, has his arm loosely around his shoulder; the way men do without being gay-looking. They are in front of a snooker table at the holiday camp near Brighton that we went to every year. I took the photos then, as that week I was dreaming of being a fashion photographer. I had turned the camera to a forty-five-degree angle and pressed the button without care and then wound it on very fast and took another shot, winding it on speedily again, making my thumb hurt on the grooves, wishing I had an automatic.

Simon is missing.

There is a poster with his face on it outside the police station. I pass it every morning on my way to Ruby's caff, where I work, and know that it doesn't look anything like him. It says underneath:

HAVE YOU SEEN THIS MAN?

Simon Rodgerson has been missing for three months. He has brown eyes and brown hair, is 23 years old, slim build and 6ft tall. He was last seen on Christmas Day at home when he left after a family dispute. If you have seen him please contact us.

What I would write underneath his picture is:

Simon, otherwise known as Amanda, was last seen as his mother threw him out of the house on Christmas Day with the dinner hot on the table and Simon dressed as a woman, in a wonky black bobbed wig and fake tan leather shoes that pinched him. He has lovely elegant hands but incredibly knobbly knees and is afraid the world will reject him, which it will because she did.

Mum had called him disturbed, although it was her that was disturbing him. And then when I told her I'd known for a while and that I didn't find it that strange, she didn't react at all but sat herself in your armchair, which we still have, with a bottle of sherry, staring at the label as if it were instructions on what to do next.

'Didn't I love you enough?' she had said as I packed a chocolate orange in my leaving rucksack.

And then she bent forward as if in chronic pain and cried, 'My children are both ill.'

And that was enough for me to never want to see her again, which of course would have been easy if she had not been our mother.

3

Three miles away, two bus changes, past a chained-up dog who doesn't bark and a short cut through the park where men rustle in the bushes at night, is where she lives. He sleeps there too with his fat neck. Exactly where I had slept, I bet. She always liked the side by the door, more roomy she'd said.

For twenty-one days now Sally has been my ex-girlfriend and there are still no signs of her stalking me, so I am up the road from her house behind the tree watching her double-glazed porch. So far, she hasn't rung and put the phone down when I pick it up and she hasn't begged me on my doorstep to take her back. Every song on the radio means something to me so I have taken out the batteries.

She is acting like she never cared at all.

It took just one night for me to fall in love and then nine weeks for her to tell me it wasn't working and that I couldn't give her what she wanted as 'You don't have a penis, you do realise?' or words to that effect.

I had tried to ignore her late-night phone calls as she whispered and giggled in the bathroom with the taps on full. Biting my tongue, not wanting to know but straining to hear anyway, my stomach shifting at the constant arrival of new text messages, beeping and vibrating on the kitchen worktops. Without having to be in the same room, I could hear her fingers, silently, expertly texting back and I kept my hand over my mouth so that my heart wouldn't jump out.

Relationships are about trust, so the magazine Agony Aunt I'd written to had said. She'd replied that I didn't have any hard evidence not to trust Sally and maybe I should look at myself and whether I had something called low self-esteem. And I was very conscious that I didn't want to have that, so I ignored the distance in her eyes and how she slept with her back to me.

When I touched her it was as if she held her breath until I was finished.

And on her birthday, when I should have been sticking pastel-coloured candles into their pastel flower-shaped holders, I had tried not to look at things I shouldn't have. I didn't want to be jealous or overreact and I thought I was doing ever so well until I found myself spying on her, that evening, in the pub across the way from where she issued British passports.

4

Not washed, but dressed in last night's clothes, the stranger sits on my sofa nursing a mug of tea, her annoying wavy hair tucked behind her ears. She is staring, motionless, at the telly which is not on and I try to ignore her, hoping she will take the uncomfortable hint.

The clock is ticking louder than normal so I put the radio on to silence it. The radio doesn't work and then I recall hiding the batteries from myself. Instead I open up the kitchen window to let the outside in.

A car boot shuts, a child yells and a plane flies over oddly low in the echoey blue sky and my hangover claps over my eyes as if someone has tied an elastic band around my brain. I stand at the kitchen sink and wash up the glasses left from the night before. We must have had a drink when we came in. Two glasses stand neatly next to one another by the sink. The stranger must have put them there as I would have left them on the floor. There is a cigarette butt in the British Rail ashtray. One of your stolen ashtrays.

I am wearing my Christmas present from the year before last, a luxury white towelling gown, the sort that only stays white if you never wear it or if it is hung in hotel rooms. I had asked Mum for it and she had splashed out. Across my chest I can feel a tightness as I can see the girl on the sofa never leaving (there is no wall dividing my kitchen from the lounge) and us being married, her staring down at her slippers and mentioning through a mouth full of something home-made that we haven't had sex for a month.

The stranger does go in the end, rather awkwardly and without asking for my number. Although I didn't want her to have it I was offended that she hadn't asked.

As soon as I see the girl turn the corner of my road from the kitchen window (she hadn't looked back, meaning she wasn't in love with me), I rush down to the flat below, still in my dressing gown, to see Petula, the only friend I still have from school, who had given me the wink when the old couple died leaving the flat empty.

I tap on the door and let myself in with the key Petula has given me in case she accidentally dies in her sleep. I am impatient to tell her that my winking practice had paid off the previous night and that the girl has just left. My hair isn't brushed and all of a sudden as I close the door to Petula's flat I am feeling like that stud from the middle of the night (even though I wasn't sure what we had got up to).

At last I have my audience, but once in the kitchen I find Petula in her tartan pyjamas and Jackie O black sunglasses at the kitchen table staring at a letter. It is from Ewan, her secret boyfriend, the words written with great force creating a sort of Braille on the flip side of the page. My winning moment is spoilt.

Without looking at me, she lifts up the letter. I read it in my head; it is one of his poems scribbled in sloped handwriting in blue biro.

'Pickled Onions'

I am a pickled onion in a jar
Left alone at the swinging party
And through the sour vinegary brown haze
I look on at the sociable crisps and peanuts
And the popular short-lived lives of sausage rolls
Quicker than the life of an ice cube.

After the revellers have gone I'm
Shut away again in the dark of the fridge

And Time passes, until
The pregnant woman dips her fingers in
And crunches me
Sucking the bitter juice off her fingers.

And I am broken down
To begin again
In the belly of a child
Who is left alone at parties.

Then there is a little note at the bottom of the page which says:

I can't bear it any longer so I've gone to Wales to find my inner Dylan.

Thanks, Petula, you were lovely. Ewan xxx

I have heard lots about Ewan but I've never actually met him. I know he is Welsh and a depressed part-time unpublished poet who designs wallpaper for a living. And I am told he is insatiable in bed. But insatiable to Petula sounds a bit rough to me. He likes to throw her against the wall and speak all gravelly like he is in a French film. Once, he asked her to wear a beret before she began a blow job. He smokes Gitanes; I can smell them sometimes in my flat. From the start they've had a stormy relationship and Petula has never explained exactly why I can't meet him, except that I won't like him. She has six rolls of his wallpaper. They are all plain and I have spent much time studying them, trying to imagine how someone can design patternless wallpaper all day.

'Stupid bastard,' she says, as I sit down in the chair opposite her. 'It's the best thing he's ever written.' She starts to cry and holds her head in her hands, her hair pouring between her fingers.

I want to tell my story but, 'Do you think he'll be back?' I say.

'It's too late,' she says, pulling her sunglasses back onto her head, revealing bloodshot eyes. 'He took back the six rolls of wall-paper last night.'

And that is that, Ewan has won.

The day is going to be all about him. I make tea which should have eased the situation, except Petula stands up and empties her mug of tea down the sink and gets out a bottle of vodka from her pasta cupboard and pours it into the mug without rinsing the tea out first. This is unlike her as normally she is very hygienic.

'You see, I knew this would happen,' she says, looking up. 'I bet he goes on to be the next Poet Laureate or something. I have always felt that I am destined to live the life of an artist's wife. I thought all his other poems were shit until this one. I mean, he sat feeling what it was like to be a pickled onion. It's so deep.'

'Look,' I say. Can I possibly get a snippet of last night in?

'I know what you're going to say, Lizzie,' she says, swigging at the mug. 'You're gonna say at the end of the day it wouldn't have worked out anyway. You're gonna say that his nose was too big and that he smelt funny and I'm a sex addict whose life is totally out of control.'

'I wasn't going to say any of that. I never met him, remember?' I say.

She pours more vodka into her mug.

'You're gonna say it's because he reminded me of Dad and I want to sleep with someone who reminds me of my long-lost cheating father and accuse me of incest and all sorts. But you see . . . he was nothing like Dad apart from the holes in the socks and the way he likes his home cooking.'

She looks at me and says, 'I didn't sleep with my father before he left if that's what you're thinking.'

I'm not thinking at all. Considering I have known Petula for over fourteen years I am continuously surprised how little she does know of what I think.

The vodka bottle is making me feel sick. I am sat somewhere within myself as if I have layers of lard coating my skin and am about to swim the Channel. Protected by the morning-after numbness, I have a flashback of the stranger weeing outside the house in between two parked cars. She hadn't pulled down her jeans far enough and it had ended up going all inside of them, and because I was too drunk, I hadn't particularly cared. I start to think about crossing the Channel at night and how you'd be glad of anyone else's urine to keep you warm and how you might see a whale like Tom Hanks did in that *Cast Away* film and you would become friends who could communicate without speech or vodka.

'It's not far to Swansea, is it? Do you think I should go after him?' she says, suddenly brightening up. Petula works for a travel agent. She can get cheap deals.

'Yeah,' she says sitting up straight, her eyes tracing the wall upwards, 'I could go wearing my green neckscarf. The one he said was the same beautiful colour as the Welsh hills.'

The drink in my body is now making me feel shaky. I haven't eaten anything since the rushed beans on toast before going out.

'Look, Petula, why don't we go into the lounge and we can watch a video and I'll make us a roast dinner with Yorkshire pudding and garlic bread.' And in my mind the Yorkshire pudding puffing and swelling and the garlic bread browning and dripping in her gas oven fills my heart with a rare satisfied feeling, something like being at home, as I recall it.

The oven timer jolts me with its piercing beep just as Tippi Hedren playing Marnie has washed the black out of her hair, returning it to blonde, and locked the remains of that identity in a suitcase in a locker at a train station and pushed the key, with her foot, down the grate of a drain. It is Simon's favourite Hitchcock film and I am reminded why by the huge number of handbags and identity swaps that go on during the film. It's all insides and outsides and how Marnie just wants to be able to rest her head on her mother's knee.

Petula falls asleep face downwards on the sofa, one foot nearly touching the carpet, just as the colour red flashes on the screen and Marnie has a turn in Sean Connery's office. In the kitchen I scrape the knob-ends of the garlic bread into the bin and eat the last bit of Yorkshire pudding from Petula's plate. After clearing her kitchen up and hiding the vodka behind the cereal boxes I return to the lounge with a glass of water for her.

I stroke the hair from off her face and I kneel down beside her, placing the water on the floor below her head. Separating the strands over her ear, I bend over and whisper, 'Last night someone wanted me. They came home and stayed all night.'

Her breathing stops for a bit and I wait until it deepens again before letting myself out.

5

We are on Brighton Pier, poking our heads through the holes. Simon is a mermaid and I am a diver. We thought it would be funny that way round, uncanny now with the way things have turned out. We are standing on tiptoes and our chins are straining to stay in the holes. Mum took the photo and managed to get it all in this time. I can remember her leather handbag on her shoulder, with a packet of mints and travel tissues in it, always there as if they bred themselves. The travel tissues used to smell of mints as if they'd had an affair.

It felt like it was the first sunny day of the year. Maybe because it was the first day we saw Mum laugh for a long time. She was laughing as she took the picture as there is a little camera jolt to remind me. Then there is an underexposed photo of me beside some fruit machines. You can see three gold bells lit up above three red cherries and I am the dark figure in front smiling. That week, I wanted to work on the pier behind the plastic window that says 'change' above it, giving out stacks of two- and ten-pence pieces in exchange for pound coins, surrounded by the lights of the fruitees and the smell of hot doughnuts and chips.

But then again that week, at home, I also wanted to be a cleaner at the office where Mum worked. Simon and I had to go with her after six when all the workers had gone home. It was in the paper factory round the corner and we were allowed to take home any leftover paper which had gone wrong. We could never work out what was wrong with it apart from it was peach- or green-coloured and never white. It was our drawing paper. I would swing round in the manager's black leather chair and Simon would sit at the desk outside lightly touching the keyboard of the secretary's electric typewriter, imagining it was on, playing with her pencils in the pot.

Then some nights we would collect a bag of chips from the fish and chip shop to take home to have with fried eggs and baked beans. Mum always remembered a plastic-lined bag for the pickup. As we walked back, I liked holding the bag as it felt grown up and also if you hugged the bag to yourself it was hot and a bit sweaty, like another person would get if you hugged them for too long. Once, the Chinese man behind the counter wrapped up a large piece of cod in batter and a buttered crusty roll for Simon on his birthday. There was a fruit machine in the fish and chip shop which we were forbidden to touch as it was only supposed to be a seaside thing. Also chips weren't allowed to be eaten in the street at home whereas they could be by the seaside with wooden forks.

We would go down to Brighton at least twice a summer on the train, as well as the week at the holiday camp. It was where Simon and me put on our first eyeshadow, a smoky blue colour, in the wet sandy-floored toilets under the pier. Mum was sat on the pebbles minding the picnic. Simon had snatched the eyeshadow from me as soon as I had smeared it onto my eyelids. I'd watched him plant his finger into the pot and close his eyes and stroke his eyelid with his forefinger. I watched the other children watch him as I squirmed. As soon as Mum noticed she got out a tissue and with her spit rubbed it off of us, saying we were too young and then, looking at Simon, that it was only for girls anyway. He ran off and threw pebbles into the sea while I had a sausage roll. But, between the application and her discovery of the eyeshadow, we'd both walked separately out of the toilets along the promenade, me first, like models, to see who would watch us. I saw a man stare at me and pretended that I hadn't. Then I heard some jeering and ran back to pull Simon away from a group of older boys. From somewhere we knew that if we were looked at it made us successful, that we were winners of a game we could only guess at.

Was that the same day that I cut my foot on the pebbles and blood appeared in my knickers? Would you even know that from where you are? Simon was jealous that I had special packages wrapped in little plastic envelopes bought for me; I think he used to take them and hide them or wear them.

It was all very secretive and annoying.

6

Nine weeks with Sally, and the magical morning was just the same as it had always been. The alarm set for seven went off at seven. I rolled over and kissed her back, her seven o'clock kiss. She'd turned over, still asleep, and loosely draped her arm across my ribs. Waking quickly, I'd examined her face with my eyes and noticed one white eyelash over her left eye that I'd never seen before. When had this appeared? Can this sort of thing happen overnight or had I not been observing? Then there was the new growth of tiny black hairs by her eyebrows, soon to be plucked, no doubt. A spot had surfaced on her chin, only faintly swollen though. It might not come to anything.

She opened her eyes and turned away sighing. Suddenly, it felt wrong to be looking at her.

It was her birthday and I'll tell you now that I've always liked birthdays.

So, I got up and fed her lazy fish downstairs and pulled back the curtains, watching for the postman. He wore short sleeves all year round and appeared always rosy-faced, a clear sign of an alcoholic. Only the eternal optimist (or the child) likes the rattle of the letter box and letters still excited me, especially ones with handwritten addresses on the front. It reminds me that people are still using pens. But since nobody knew I was there I wasn't about to get anything good.

I switched on the kettle and then the oven and took the card out of my bag. It was her birthday, but also our anniversary. It was nine weeks today since we'd met and soon it would be three months, a whole quarter of a year. Maybe then who knows? A year, forever?

Above the kitchen ceiling I could hear her feet padding around her bedroom.

'Stay in bed!' I shouted up the stairs and I heard her get back into bed and the beep of her mobile phone as she turned it on. The kettle had finished boiling and there were three more beeps, which signalled messages had arrived, before I'd got the tea bags in the mugs. No doubt birthday messages, one from her mother and two from the tennis club maybe.

As a treat I had bought and then hidden behind the sofa a packet of four pains au chocolat from Marks & Spencer's. While I was thinking about what to write in her card, I took the pastries out of the wrapper and put them in the oven. The card was a cartoon of a penguin surrounded by the night sky looking into a hole in the ice. It was silly, I know, but underneath the ice you could see all the fishes having a wild party. Some were wearing eyeshadow and smoking cigarettes. Two had bras on and there was a table with little fish nibbles and Martini cocktails. The light was all yellowy and warm compared to the dark night sky above the ice. Sally loved penguins.

To my Sally,
Happy 33rd Birthday . . .
Yours forever xxxx

I put the pen down and decided against tea. Today was a coffee day, not instant but a cafetière day, a day to take a bit of time over, pore over, like my love for her. Sliding the card into the silvery envelope I licked the gum and realised I hadn't yet cleaned my teeth. Some days the fuzzy taste of sleep in your mouth is worse than on others, more eggy and rancid, but today was a good day, not too much taste on the tongue and nearly no aroma.

Yet time was short. She would soon have to be in the shower and dressed in her grey pinstripe suit. I had got it from the dry-cleaner's yesterday along with a bunch of daffodils from the stall by the butcher's.

As I walked up the stairs, I started humming the Happy Birthday tune quietly, thinking I would rise to a full singing version by the time I'd reached the bedroom. On the breakfast tray were the four pains au chocolat on a plate, her card, a daffodil in a little tiny vase like they do in pizza restaurants and the proud unplunged cafetière with two cups.

The bedroom door was shut. My two hands were on the tray and there was not another to open the door.

So, I put the tray down on the wooden floor and swung the door open. Sally was stood in front of the wardrobe mirror naked, her hands on her hips, examining her body. Her bottom was facing me, small and pert, not really a trace of cellulite to be seen.

I started to hum the Happy Birthday tune again and brought in the tray and squashed a square of white duvet with it.

She hadn't turned round by this point and was putting on her Japanese-style silk dressing gown with the tie around her waist knotted tightly.

'Come back to bed. You've got to open your card. The postman hasn't been yet,' I said.

She turned round but didn't face me. Her head was turned to the side and she was staring through the bedside lamp and she breathed in heavily as if she was about to announce something. Then she glanced at the tray and looked at me and then away.

'Oh,' she said. 'I haven't really got time, I've got to get in the shower.'

'Oh come on,' I said. 'It's not every day it's your birthday, is it? And I've never got to share it with you before.' I patted the bed, then I pushed the plunger on the cafetière down, watching her out of the corner of my eye. Coming towards me, she picked up the card and opened it.

She sort of smiled at the picture of the penguin and I felt pleased that I'd made her happy, but still she didn't give me that look I was waiting for or the kiss I'd expected. The thank-you kiss you get for doing something thoughtful for someone.

And then she'd left the room with a coffee in her hand and I was sitting on the bed feeling the tears fizz in my nose. I could smell antiseptic wipes although there were none in the room. The breakfast tray began to swim on the bed and it was all too much to think about and I know I shouldn't have done it and I know when characters in soap operas do it you know it's wrong, but it was irresistible.

Her mobile phone was on the bedside table.

And I knew she was in the shower for as long as it takes to shave her daily legs.

She was washing her hair as there were splats of water shooting against the shower curtain and I knew I had to have at least a few minutes before she'd dried herself and her hair with the towel, brushed through the knots, tied a towel up in a turban and rubbed in the expensive body lotion which the report in the magazine says contains the same substance as explosives.

So there it was:

Messages
Inbox

S
happy birthday can still smell u
on my skin from last nite wonna
do it again tonight?:-) am hard
thinking about u c u later xx

Messages
Sent
P

hello u feel the same too don't
wanna shower in case I can't smell
ur sweat on me meet after work
and I want a surprise! ;-) xxx

7

Ruby's caff is called Ruby's Cafe. I calculate it was there when you were around, wasn't it? The sign above it doesn't have an accent over the e like the French do as she is from round here and she says she thinks that would be pretentious.

I am across the street from the police station on the way to work and I can see Simon's face in the glass box next to the normal faded crime prevention pictures and advice on window locks.

But today there is a new picture there and I cross the traffic lights to see it, not waiting for the green man. Simon's HAVE YOU SEEN picture has been moved to the left and in the centre now is a photocopy of a young girl's face. She is eighteen years old and has been missing for five weeks. HAVE YOU SEEN HER? She has mousy brown hair tied back really tightly from her face making it appear moonlike. She is not smiling and Simon is not smiling either. In fact, they both look miserable together in the locked box and I wonder if their glares would soften a little if instead they were pinned to trees, free to flap in the wind like the signs for missing cats.

Walking away, I focus on the Turkish man stacking boxes of vine-ripened tomatoes outside his shop. I never think he will sell them all, but because they taste of real tomatoes I think he does. Petula loves his marinated olives. I used to go in there to buy Turkish bread to take back to Sally's after work, thinking it was exotic. The Turkish women on the tills wear sugar-pink lipstick and have their hair blow-dried and sprayed perfectly. They dress up to come to work and look as though they are enjoying themselves, as if they are old-fashioned air hostesses. The first time I presented her with the sesame flatbread Sally's eyes lit up as she took in the hugeness of it. We laughed about how long it would take to eat. I imagined us starting at each end and ending up in the middle, kissing like they do in the ads.

Every time I took that journey to Sally's I was nervous, all the way there, stomach spilling over on every turn of the bus, not being able to breathe, trying to think of calm things like a pond without any wildlife on it. Now I don't feel anything. Maybe that's why she left me, because I was too nervous on the bus? But how would she know unless that panicky bus journey was still there on my lips when I kissed her hello. I haven't been back to the shop since we split up; it's bad enough I have to walk past it every morning.

As always, Ruby is there an hour before she flips back the closed sign to open, preparing the lunchtime special behind the case of warming pies. I wave at her to unlock the door and take in my last grease-free breath and there is a faint salty promise of the sea in the air, up from the south, from Brighton maybe.

'Hello, love. You had a good night?' She smiles her smile, her eyes crinkling up to match the skin on her chest. She is forking over the mashed potato on a large shepherd's pie.

'Yes, fine.' (I got in after midnight, waiting until I knew Sally had gone to bed.)

'You heard from Petula again? Has she spotted Wallpaper Ewan? God, she must be serious. I can't believe she'd be so daft as to go and look for him though. Well, on second thoughts, I suppose, in the nicest possible way, she always has had a bit of a screw loose, hasn't she?'

Then she tilts her face up at me, her kind cow eyes underlined with black kohl eye pencil, stopping the fork motion on the mashed potato.

'I hope you tried to put her off?'

Thinking about it, I hadn't actually done that much to dissuade her. After all, I was preparing the roast and I know that sometimes you can't help but pursue love even when it's officially over; your heart doesn't let you.

At the kitchen table Petula had sat drinking, going through the multiple possibilities of why he'd gone.

'Maybe it was his love for Wales which had increased his hatred of south London,' she'd said, drawing circles around the vodka bottle lid with her finger. Then she'd gone on to list his reasons for going, which were:

1. The lack of magic mushrooms last autumn.
2. The lack of green hills to enjoy the effects of the magic mushrooms.
3. The lack of Welsh people in south London.
4. The lack of Poetry Unplugged nights in the vicinity (not that he'd looked that hard).
5. She lives here.

And lastly, the big one, the one she especially liked to dwell on because it made her feel especially bad, was

6. She hadn't satisfied him with his abnormally high sex drive.
7. She hadn't satisfied him with his abnormally high sex drive.
8. She hadn't satisfied him with his abnormally high sex drive.
9. She hadn't satisfied him with his abnormally high sex drive.

Instead of troubling Ruby with these details I give her a compliment.

'Did I tell you I made the Yorkshire pudding the way you told me to on Sunday, plain flour and don't open the oven door for the first twenty minutes? It was lovely.' (When it first came out it looked like a baked landscape seen from a plane window.)

'Are you all right, Lizzie?' Ruby's eyebrows are touching the tips of her mascaraed eyelashes, all stiffly coated. She will never lose them into the food while on duty.

I hate it when she probes me. It makes me feel as if I am wearing my life on my face, like the women in the high street who shout 'fuckin' shut up' at their kids in pushchairs, their faces set hard, their mouths turned down with cigarettes drooping out, their eyes bolted shut.

I roll up my coat and place it in a carrier bag so that it doesn't pick up the smell of the deep-fat fryer.

'I worry about you, love. Your life is so unsettled.' Which when translated means she is talking about you and Mum and Simon and how you left and how Mum has gone off the rails and how Simon has disappeared and how Sally is involved with a man with a fat neck.

'I'm fine, Ruby.' I use her name for added emphasis. And I would be fine as long as I could find Simon and someone to come home with me once more and discover some sign to say that Sally misses me in a small but important way.

I mean, love can't just disappear, can it, and where does it go if it does? Or does it just turn into some other feeling, like bitterness or sadness, nothing solid, just something that changes your face and makes you rip up photos?

Ruby bangs the oven door shut and turns round, wiping her hands on a cloth.

'Did you watch that programme last night called *Changing Faces: When it all goes wrong*? It was on Channel 4. Now what time was it? Well, it was after I'd spoken to Cath, so it must have been about eight. No? You didn't? Well, it was all about these silly women who just gaze in the mirror, bored, thinking their lives will be much better if they can remove a few laughter lines. More money than sense, I think ... Well, one woman ended up with the face of a rubber doll. She looked so horrible, I had to laugh. I mean, a rubber dolly face. Serves her right if you ask me. Well, let's face it, none of us are getting any younger but we don't see any of our normal old people trying to be something that they're not. It's all those Americans . . . either obsessed with how thin they can look or obsessed with getting so fat that they don't look like anything except huge marshmallows . . .' And she is off and my gaze drifts onto her smoker's mouth, lines drawing up from the lips, small channels for her lipstick to bleed into, even though she only has a couple a day. Sixty-year-old skin is obviously not self-generating.

I gaze down at Ruby's black high heels and deniered feet. Having worn high heels for so long means she can't put her heels to the ground ever again; the muscles on the backs of her legs are locked in spasm. To show me she took off her shoes one day which made her surprisingly short, and her feet were shaped as if she still had the high heels on, like the feet of dummies in shop windows.

Ruby does not match the surroundings and the surroundings do not match each other, even though she chose the fittings herself. The problem is that she likes to update a little at a time, ending up with what the design people on the TV would call a mishmash of ideas. The chairs are dark and wooden with hand holes at the top for pulling backwards and they have plum-coloured brushed velour padded seats that hide most stains. The floor is quite new, laminated in a slightly lighter mock wood. There is real wood panelling from the seventies which reaches halfway up the walls, and above that a series of photographs of the surrounding area when there were trams. The walls are painted salmon pink and the tables are modern silver ones more suited to a café with an accent above the e. We cover these up with plastic wipe-clean checked tablecloths. Our tea is served in mugs on saucers with the tea bag left in the mug for the old people, as they like to choose how strong to have it.

The ketchup bottles need to be filled up, so do the salt and pepper shakers. Ruby hands over an old ice-cream tub of warm soapy water and a cloth and I sit for ten minutes wiping the dried sauce from the spouts of the red and brown squirters and pouring salt and brown pepper into very small holes. The old people we get in here don't like black pepper.

Then it's eight o'clock and Ruby flips the sign round and not a lot happens for a minute or so. Then, as regular as clockwork, Elsie pushes open the door, which starts the day for us and within ten minutes a few regulars are sat alone looking down at their newspapers, leaning back occasionally to gaze over at the bar where Ruby stands buttering bread or frying bacon. The radio is on and because Ruby knows what's happened to me she has switched from the usual love-music channel to a classical one.

We like it as it seems to make work a little more dramatic and not so sentimental. We work with the music turning to news once an hour and it's peculiar how little it seems to change each broadcast. Today the French girl found dead in the park (who died because she got off at the wrong bus stop) is repetitively dead, every hour she is dead.

We serve traditional caff food with a daily special which normally costs under a fiver and includes a pudding. I serve and Ruby cooks. Some of the clientele smell a bit fusty but we don't turn anyone away, we just have strategically placed air fresheners where they like to sit. And they all have their spots.

Alf sits in the corner near the window arranging his bets for the day. Elsie, who never takes her coat off and is slowly going bald, sits near us at the bar so she can earwig on our conversation. Hilda in her elasticated-waist trousers comes in daily, but on a Monday with her pension she has two puddings, and Bert sits as far away from everyone as he can. Cyril shoves half-slices of bread into his mouth all at once and it's hard to watch without feeling queasy as his teeth come a bit loose, and Hilda and Mary sit together for company with their purses on the table. No one speaks much but there is the occasional bout of laughter to remind us that they are all alive.

Half an hour into this morning and we've got Alf and Elsie in plus a strange-looking woman who has never been here before.

Elsie is reading the *Sun* and is stuck hovering over page 2 with a small magnifying glass held up close to her reading glasses. Her glasses look as though she has had them for years, as they have scratched thick lenses and heavy brown frames.

'New shirt, Alf?' I comment as I place his tea to the side of him. It is peach and there are square creases on the back where he has just taken it out of the plastic wrapping that morning.

'Yeah. Cos I'm going on holiday tomorrow.'

'Oh yes, Thailand, isn't it?'

'Yes. I'm going to collect my bride.' His eyes drift off over the caff walls to who knows where in Thailand.

'Gosh, how exciting. How did you meet?' I say.

'My son found her on the Internet for me. Something for my old age,' he says, pouring sugar in his tea.

'Usual?' I say, and he nods, glancing up at me from the racing page of his newspaper. He has watery blue eyes and a big red nose from the pub.

The woman we've never seen before has ordered a bacon sandwich and is facing the window, head lowered, face resting on her fist. She has a tattoo of a daisy at the top of her plump arm and visible bra straps which cut into her flesh. Her hair is orangey ginger. Ruby nodded at me when she'd come in, pointing her eyes as if to say look at her.

I give her the bacon sandwich with a serviette tucked under it, no cutlery needed, and she doesn't look up. She is smoking extra long cigarettes, but not in a French way. Most people stub out their cigarettes when their food arrives but she doesn't, she just continues to smoke, blowing it down onto the white bread and still not looking up. Maybe she's blind and she hasn't seen me. I step back to the table and try to slide the plate away so that I can put it down with a slam this time, but as I go to touch it she grabs my hand and I let go. Of course she's not blind; she hasn't got a dog or a stick with her. And it's horrible she should grab my hand instead of the plate or the sandwich.

'Undercover police,' Ruby whispers when I get back to the counter. 'Ob-serv-ing,' she mouths.

'Why?' I mouth back.

'Who knows?' she shrugs and I pick up the fried-egg sandwich for Elsie who is pretending not to have noticed our silent conversation.

'Here you go, Elsie,' I say sliding the plate in front of her and giving her a knife and fork rolled in a white serviette. She taps my hand.

'FBI,' Elsie mouths up at me.

Ruby and Elsie watch a lot of crime TV and they belong to the local neighbourhood watch scheme. Elsie carries spare window stickers in her bag. She gave me one when I moved into my flat but I didn't think a small bit of sticky plastic on my kitchen window would deter a burglar so I threw it away. Elsie swears by them and claims she is actively bringing down crime. She said the other day that the stickers in her handbag keep the handbag safe too, and she'd bet that if she left her bag on the bus it would be returned back to her untouched (in fact, she never lets it out of her sight). She is also a practising psychic so would probably be able to find it anyhow.

No one joins the not-blind woman with the tattoo and she leaves me a tip which surprises us all. When I go over to the table there is a dull fifty-pence piece on the edge of the plate with the half-eaten sandwich and a bus ticket lying on top of the ashtray with four cigarette stubs in it. On the ticket the word 'bus' with two question marks is written in a black biro (I put this in my pocket).

At one o'clock Elsie has finished her paper and is into the *People's Friend*, and once again the French girl got off at the wrong bus stop and was murdered in the park.

Ruby and I sit down with leftover shepherd's pie and mugs of tea. The end of my working day is getting closer and I feel a sense of panic growing deep under my belt.

8

Today is sliding away.

Not much is happening outside her double-glazed porch. I've taken four exposures already of the house. I hadn't really noticed before how ugly it is.

A thick tree only slightly thinner than my shoulders is hiding me from the porch. So is my black trench coat, a size too small, so my wrists feel the cool air of the evening, but it's all the charity shop had. I have borrowed Petula's blow-job beret and I think it suits me.

In the distance, further up the hill at the end of her road, behind some other houses and the Crystal Palace tower, the sun is setting red like it does on holiday programmes behind smug presenters.

The exterior of Sally's house is blemished. Obviously someone, a porch salesman, or woman, before I knew her, showed her a catalogue and she'd said yes. Then they'd attached a rectangular box onto the front of her house where there was once a nice open porch and she had written them a cheque. Neither one of them had taken into consideration her Victorian features.

In my detective's bag, which is my old rucksack, I have my 35mm automatic, some cheese-and-onion sandwiches on white crusty bread in tinfoil I made at work, a notebook, a black biro, my mobile phone switched off, keys to my flat and an unread post-card from Petula. She is in Wales searching for Ewan and I'd saved it for this moment when I knew I'd have a lot of time. She has been gone for four days now and she's used up all her holiday leave by going.

On one side of the postcard is a Welsh lady in national costume and Petula's handwriting is on the other.

Hello you, it's me. I have tried eating this Welsh seaweed but it sticks to your teeth and tastes of mud. No sign of Ewan but the landlady at the B&B says that the photo of him looks a bit like her dead cousin. Am heading for the Brecon Beacons as he once mentioned them in one of his poems ... Don't hold out much hope though. Remember to water the plants. I'll be back Saturday.

Love Petula x

She wouldn't be impressed that I was outside Sally's house.

She would say I was crazy and could be locked up and I had to move on, but after all, she was the one in Wales using up all her holiday.

Twenty minutes later and I have drawn multiple boxes and swirls in my notebook, a beard on the Welsh woman on the post-card and turned my mobile phone on and off twice to check the time. There is only the crust left wrapped in the sandwich foil and I've taken a photo of a bird's nest in the tree above me.

And then I can hear her voice, laughing, and I drop down to the ground, squatting behind the tree and a parked red car. My heart is banging against my coat.

'Yeah probably,' she says and laughs again and I remember her laugh and how you could hear it across a room and know she was there even if you were in the next room.

And then I hear the double-glazed porch door open and close and there is a loud silence. There are no birds chirping, no cars driving, nothing moves and I can smell the old dogshit that is under the tree by my foot. I open my bag and take out the camera, removing the camera lens, putting it in the bag. I stand up and look at her house through the lens, pressing my finger on the button halfway down so that it focuses. The flashlight flips on momentarily, lighting up the area in front of me. I take my finger off the button fast and turn off the automatic flash feature.

The bright hall light has come on and then the bedroom one comes on too, almost synchronised. Maybe the light from the two will be enough to get a photo. But then the man who smokes a lot of pot comes out of his house next to hers and I pull back behind the tree, holding the camera close to my chest. It's already dark now. He whistles off up the street and I feel nervous. I don't want to be caught on the first night, not before I have worked out if they are really in love or if it is just a thing.

And then there he is, with his fat neck, in the bedroom pulling the curtains, the curtains that I have pulled many times, the ones that have my fingerprints on too.

I take a photo of the pulled curtains, having missed him, as I was too busy staring at him with his fat neck in his safe comfy ribbed jumper and his casual jeans holding his disgusting penis.

After the lounge light has come on I walk across the street towards the house knowing that they won't be able to see me outside. If they try to look out of that window they will see only their own reflections, eating dinner on the lap trays next to each other on the sofa. The candle I bought jumping on the mantelpiece. If they look out later they will see only their own entwined image lying on the sofa, chatting and kissing and looking like any other couple in the first throes of love.

But if she did look out, away from him, at some point in the evening; if her mind wandered to when I was sat in that same dip of the beige sofa, she wouldn't see me, and even if she did, would she know who I was since I don't recognise myself any more?

9

Right now, next to an open packet of ginger biscuits, I have a Polaroid I took of Simon and our old cocker spaniel, Suzy. He has put the dog's ears up behind her head to form a hairstyle. Small tendrils of blonde hair have fallen around her face and made her look girlish even though she'd just had a hysterectomy.

Simon is wearing Mum's green eyeshadow and lip gloss, kneeling beside Suzy in a peach top. She is laughing-panting (which has been scientifically proven to be real dog happiness, so they say) and Simon has a girl's hairdo too, a mullet. It wasn't the fashion then. Surfwear was, I think.

I want to slit it open. The thickness of the photo means it must have something underneath, something in between. I want to see what's below Simon and the dog, to find out what's there. I mustn't destroy it though, so I won't, as it might be all that's left. So I just press it around the edges. I haven't heard a thing from him or Mum.

Putting the photo under my arm to develop itself was so satisfactory; no need to wait for the crunchy envelope to drop through the letter box (even though that was exciting too). I would watch the dull grey square become coloured, gradually seeing framed what I'd just seen. It made that moment more real, more real than the actual moment, more there, like underlining it with a thick pen, a whole slice of time.

Cocker spaniels stop and sniff all the time. They see in black and white but can smell in Technicolor. Every lager can, base of tree, crisp packet, has a whiff attached to a previous time. I always thought it would be wonderful to be able to smell the past on an object, to find out its history. Perhaps the screwed-up crisp packet had the hand of a child in it hungry from swimming and the crushed can of lager was secretly drunk by an alcoholic thinking of a lost chance on their way home from work. Outside our front door, the tomcats used the post as a place to compete to see whose pong would be on it last before sunrise; even someone with a cold would smell that.

Suzy had to know all the stories and it used to make me cross. Getting her to the park was an effort in itself. But Simon seemed to understand her; she was his dog really. He claimed her as soon as you'd brought her home in the car when she didn't stop running up and down the hall for ages, you remember? It was a surprise. You were wearing a winter coat and I can't see your face now, there's just hair, your black hairstyle from the photo next to Mum's bed. The winter coat was black or grey, I can't recall, or had you taken off the coat and draped it over your arm? Mum was still in her dressing gown and on the phone upstairs. That is more of a certainty than a memory as she always was in that spot when anything was happening. When she came down she gave you one of her looks and you both went into the kitchen and slid the door closed. The moment was all messed up. There were raised voices and all I could hear was her shouting at you saying 'another thing to look after' or something like that, but I could have got that wrong. I can only recollect that the dog's arrival was not a welcome one and that it was very close to when you left.

Suzy was always in Simon's room after you went. I know he used to dress her up and would have put make-up on her if she didn't have fur all over her skin. I was left with the solitary cat that didn't like me watching her dig her holes in the garden.

Or have I made all this up? I'm reminded of the day we cut off the dog's eyelashes and the cat's whiskers because by the time they'd grown back you'd gone.

10

However hard I try I always cook enough for four which makes me ask, who are the three other people I am cooking for? Petula manages a small mouthful sometimes which helps out, but what if I'm cooking for the husband and two children I'll never have? Or is it you, Mum and Simon? Or is it the three stooges, muses, dimensions, faces of Eve, or the three degrees? We were once a two-point-four family.

Black jumpers are slimming they say. I have a dark purple one on which I presume will have the same effect. It is after work and I washed the grease smell off of me and then the dishes after cooking spaghetti bolognese for the mystery guests and I am in a corner of a new bar called the G-Spot. I couldn't have stayed in. Petula is away and I want someone to come home with me, I need someone else to be there.

Sally is swirling around my head making me feel drunk. She would be cooking their tea, with him beside her, kissing in between letting him taste the sauce off the wooden spoon. Laughing, he would put his hairy fingers on her back, grab her breast with his other manly hand then lift her onto the kitchen surfaces and thrust himself into her, making the cutlery drawer rattle and gasp, the dinner bubbling out of control and the saucepan lids lifting up releasing coughs of steam.

Before leaving the house I threw three wine glasses on the floor one by one until I felt better. I had to get the Hoover out before I left though, wincing at the thought of a shard of glass in my foot.

An overground train with no ticket machine at the station brought me to the Tube station. I had to buy a permit to travel, which is basically where you put in ten pence and hope no one stops you and makes you pay the full fare. On the train, a man, a woman and a dog came out of the toilet. It was clear that they had been taking drugs in there and the dog was panting hard as it pulled out of the narrow space. They walked into the next carriage leaving a dirty yellow smell behind them. The old woman opposite me pulled her bag closer to her.

The moon is a bold boiled egg in the sky.

From the train station I walk round the corner with my hand in my bag touching your old A–Z just in case I feel nervous. An A–Z always makes me feel better even if I know where I am, as it makes sense of things. The Tube station is opposite the cinema which is now a pub. It had a quick run as a bingo hall.

My breasts feel heavy as if someone has pumped them up with air. I wish I had a valve to let them down a bit.

In the corner of the bar near the toilets I am standing near the fruit machine really wanting to have a go but not letting myself. I was only ever allowed at the seaside. Once I start I just can't stop and I don't want to give the impression that I am an alcoholic gambler.

There is someone looking at me and I stare back until I realise it is a full-length me in a full-length mirror. And I am fat. The largest I have ever been and my belly has popped out over the top of my jeans. I don't look like me. I appear like one of those before pictures in the magazines that normally have an after picture with them so it shows how much better and happier you will be when you are half the size. I am a before me.

Looking away, my gaze rests on a skinny couple sat snogging behind two empty pints of lager. One of them has her hand resting between the other one's legs which are splayed the way men do. Their jeans are not where they should be and they are showing their underpants which are like men's boxer shorts. They have short hair, spiked with gel and longer at the back, and they look the same. They have mullets like Simon did once.

They open their eyes and glance over at me with hard glares so I turn round and stand with my back to them. My hair is shoulder-length and I am conscious that I look very different to them. I can tell they are staring at me and I wonder if they find me attractive at all with my belly and bulging bottom.

The night is dead and it has a sad feeling about it, almost as if nothing good will ever happen again. That couple are the only other people in here. It's 20.07 on the face of my mobile and I attempt to strike up a conversation with the bored barmaid after ordering another Sea Breeze.

'It's quiet tonight, isn't it?' I say.

'Yeah,' she says.

'Was it busy this weekend?' I say.

'Opening night,' she says.

Too early for a wink, I think.

'Oh, I was at Push Up on Saturday. It was really good.' (A woman came home with me and I'm sure we had great sex.)

'Yeah.' And she wanders off, touching the strip of dry-roasted peanuts as she goes to the other side of the bar. Is that a sign?

I wander through the alcove to the other side and take a table in the corner in view of the barmaid and the door, which you can just about see. Three more girls arrive just before closing and I have drunk five Sea Breezes and got five more yeahs from the barmaid. She is not interested, in me or the job. During the course of the evening I have travelled along the Thames with my finger in the A–Z. There is no Tate Modern and no Dome in your edition. I promised myself I would walk along the Thames in summer and photograph what had been washed up.

Last orders got murmured and I sucked the pink melted ice out of my glass and retook the journey from four hours before, but in reverse. Tomorrow had already arrived by the time I reached my flat.

11

If she had said forget your family and that you have a history and a mind of your own and follow me, be the shadow of my dog (if she had one) and make yourself so small that you fit in the crack behind the radiator or sit still with your hands on your head till your arms shake uncontrollably, I would have said OK. After nine weeks, that's how big my love was for her.

But she didn't ask.

I brought her flowers every day, bright sunlit daffodils or deep and meaningful purple gerberas. She seemed to love it at first, placing the vase on top of the TV, my flowers in competition with *Coronation Street* and the six o'clock news. The next night's flowers went on the mantelpiece and the following days on the window ledge until it looked like it was her thirtieth birthday again, when everyone sent her flowers and I didn't know her and she was with that silly girl who once got violent on super-strength lager and left marks on her arms.

I was her audience and I wanted it to be an exclusive show for one. Towards the end the tickets were getting more expensive every day, but I didn't mind. Now they are not even on sale. Him and his fat neck have first refusal. He gives her that seven o'clock kiss with his prickly chin every morning. She'll be pregnant next as she's at that age, and what will she tell the child? Will she ever admit that she had feelings for me? It feels like they've won all over again. She's joined them. They will always win with their two-point-fourness and three-bedroom houses and whole decades of television and movies dedicated to breeding.

I am in the pub opposite Sally's work; Ruby let me go early as I complained of a headache, which wasn't an absolute lie as I could have had one. She comes here every Friday with her work people and I am going to leave as soon as she arrives. It is crucial that she sees me and thinks that I have somewhere else important to go. If only my mobile could ring at that moment.

The pub is owned by a chain and it doesn't play any music. At first it seemed strange to hear people just talking, but I'm glad there is no jukebox as I would be tempted to play Stevie Wonder songs and let my brain spiral again.

I am at the front of the raised non-smoking level near the back of the pub. She will see me as soon as she comes in. I am wearing a pink jumper so that I stand out from all the suits around about me. The clientele up here don't seem to swear as much as the people who sit in the smoking section. Personally I only like a good fuck or shit when I've stubbed my toe as it's not necessary most of the time. When I said fucking hell once, Mum said that people who swear a lot use it to cover up that they have very little to say, but I think it's a stalling device; a good smattering of fuckings in every sentence gives you more time to think about about what you are saying.

I wish Petula could be here as it would look more natural, as if we just happened to be here. But that's not really important as I want to be printed onto her mind, a quick snapshot developed in her brain, an instant Polaroid to blot out Fat Neck.

My mobile phone is on the table. It is a new one which takes pictures and I am beginning to see the benefits, although it seems extraordinary to have a phone which is other things too. It has an inbuilt tape machine so that you can record what people say, which is very handy if you are a detective. It's like having a toaster that tap-dances. People have mini porn films on them too. It's a craze like Rubik's cubes were once. Some boys on the train the other day were all huddled together laughing and groaning at what I think from their comments was an obese naked woman bouncing up and down on a man who looked like he was enjoying being crushed.

Extraordinary. What a funny word. When you call someone that it means they are unusual or remarkable but it really means the opposite to that. It's all upside down, like when you believe you are the centre of someone's world and then you find out you're not even in it.

I have given myself a headache and I am glad in a way as it means I didn't really tell Ruby a lie. It is five past six on the phone and she'll be walking in any minute. Will she see me and come over? Should I ask her to sit down and have a drink and then ask her to come away with me? Scotland is supposed to be good at this time of year and we could go and see that naked tattooed man who lives as a hermit on the Isle of Skye. Petula could get us a package deal. Even a day out in Brighton would be nice, hot doughnuts on the pier. Yes, I shall suggest a day out if we get talking and then when we go I shall be at my most charming and she will fall in love with me and forget all about Fat Neck.

The door swings open and Fat Neck walks in, holding the door open like a cliché. What is he doing here? Can't they leave each other alone? Sally follows, laughing at something he is saying. She is backlit, with the late-afternoon sun straining through her blonde hair.

Her face drops when she sees me. She grabs Fat Neck's arm and whispers to him, looking up at me. I get up and put on my coat and walk towards them. My legs feel wobbly and my mouth has dried up. They stand at the bar, unified, pretending not to look at me, and I pretend not to look at them. A heterosexual couple among millions of others. But then as I go forward I trip down the step and fall onto the patterned carpet. I fall on my face. A man in a suit helps me up, pulling at my arm, and I'm saying, I'm OK I'm OK it's fine leave me, and my face is hot and red.

My 35mm camera has fallen out on the floor and the back has swung open, exposing the film, and the suited man is trying to close it, squashing the brown film down.

It is all ruined.

12

It is nearly all ruined, until I have the idea to go back to Sally's house and find out once and for all what's going on. There must be a trace of me left in the house; I know my hair is sunk deep down her plughole, reachable by tweezers. And if Sally hasn't hoovered properly my eyelashes and skin flakes should still be there too, mixed up with theirs.

They say the body sheds a layer of skin every twenty-eight days and since it's been twenty-four days since that day when I walked into the pub and he was spooning lasagne into Sally's mouth, it means that the skin I have under my jumper, next to my bra, will have touched the skin she still has now.

We have only a few days left before our skins will not know one another.

I liked it that day when I cleaned and there was a dirty rim for me to wipe from the bath. Lemon cleaning fluid on a damp scourer prickled my nose as I scrubbed, and there were hairs in the corner on the lino mixed with fluff.

Her hair, her fluff.

Her fluff was a deep blue-grey colour with strands of blonde hair matting it all together. If I'd had enough time to collect more it could have made a tartan scarf for winter.

Under the carpet in the porch Sally keeps a spare front-door key by the electricity meter. I pray it will still be there. And will my photo still be on the fridge, held on by the Big Apple fridge magnet? The fridge magnet another girl from another time brought her back from New York. I can hardly wait for the train to pull out of the station now. We will go past the elderly Battersea Power

Station with its chimneys in the air, held up by scaffolding, soon to have a makeover, and the dogs in the home beside it watching through the metal grilles waiting for something to happen.

The guard stands on the platform with his fingers on a key that slots into the post to close the doors. He has a walkie-talkie instead of the whistle that would once have hung off his lips. A few people run on at the last minute. My knee is burning from falling on the carpet and then again I am on the floor of the pub in front of them and they are looking down at me, laughing and pointing, the amusement echoing around the optics. His fat neck is bulging with smugness as if he is wearing her on his ribbed jumper like a brash birthday badge which roars I've won.

The train is crowded, but I have a seat by the window. I have more air. My thighs are touching the man's next to me and I try to pull them in by doing that bottom clench Petula says makes it pert and is a good pelvic-floor exercise for women who have had children or simply want to keep their man satisfied. He is ignoring me and is slumped down with his eyes closed listening to his iPod. He is sitting with his legs open like those girls were in the G-Spot and I'm aware that my weight is pressing against him hard and that it's quite pleasant to have the contact. I am wondering whether he is thinking about my thigh pushed against his hip.

The train slowly leaves the concourse and I take out my camera which I think is broken. I pull the brown film out which would have had the photos of Sally's house on it. The man opposite watches me while pretending to read his newspaper. He has half-moon glasses on like a nosy owl and I want to tell him to mind his own business. The camera back won't stay shut even without any film in it. It'll cost a lot to mend.

A few things like light bulbs have broken lately. The other night I switched on the lounge light and it blew with a determined ping, the bathroom one flickered and died the same evening. I have no wine glasses left. When things break I take it personally. I remember, when inspired by a TV chef, I spent eight hours on my day off kneading and leaving dough to make my only ever loaf for Sally. The oven blew up just at the moment when it was ready to go in and I had to throw it away as it was eleven thirty at night. Why should an oven choose to do that at that moment when I was trying to make our love loaf and not when I was just reheating something?

It makes me think there are higher forces at work.

Or is it all emotional electricity like the sort which young teenage girls are charged with, their hormones so luminous they draw ghosts towards them?

Maybe I am full of that electricity and if I concentrate hard enough I could get the man opposite's spectacles to fall off his nose. I focus very hard like when you sit and look at a glass and try to get it to move across the table. He scratches his nose and that is proof enough for me. Tonight I must be filled with the power.

The train draws into Sally's nearest station and it is all too familiar. The thin graffitied platform is empty apart from the bench and the locked toilets. The iPod man pulls his legs together and to the side to let me out. He is not watching my bottom but moving his finger around on the circular pad searching for a song. I tiptoe around the knees of the other two passengers and my hips knock the shoulders along the aisle on the way to the doors. People shift touchily back in their seats and I'm glad to be off.

What used to be our local shop is run by a small Indian man. When I go up to the counter he recognises me and smiles. I put the bottle of wine with a screw top on the counter and he says, 'Hello, madam, anything else?' He always says that and I always say no.

'I've not seen you or your friend for a while,' he says. The word friend annoys me but then again how would he know what she was to me?

'No, she's been away,' I say.

'Oh, somewhere nice?' he says.

'No, nowhere in particular. Just somewhere foreign,' I say, feeling prickly about Fat Neck. I pick up the blue-and-white-striped bag which always feels too flimsy to hold bottles.

He looks at me and laughs, hoping I am making a joke. Maybe it is a joke. What would I know about foreign landscapes? If I had a map of the world on the wall and pins to mark where I'd been, three pins would probably cover it all. London (centre and south-east), Brighton and that day trip to France on the ferry on your shoulders. The Highlands of Scotland is as far away as I can imagine getting to on my wage. Though travelling abroad has never really appealed to me. They say you can travel in your own armchair (I have tried to do this without the aid of TV or magazines and once got near the Taj Mahal after I'd dropped off only because of that famous Princess Diana photograph). Plus I've flicked through the brochures Petula brings home from work and it all looks very expensive.

Sally wanted to go to South Africa to see the penguins. I mentioned that they have them at London Zoo and she looked at me as if I was joking and I laughed as if I was, but they do have them there.

The Indian man has a good selection of cheap wine in his shop; it was always worth the walk from Sally's house. On leaving the shop I unscrew the top and take a mouthful of wine. The warmth covers my chest like sunburn.

Either I choose the long way around the park to get to her house or the short cut through it. This means walking past the bushes where Sally said men wait for surprises from each other. She said it's a mixture of older married men and gay men who want to have a stranger's mouth around their cocks and it doesn't cost any money, so that's why they go, as pensions don't stretch to rent boys. Plus it must be more fun outside, I would have thought, with branches poking at you and it being ever so exciting in case you get caught.

I enter the side gate of the park. The lighting is very faint and I can see my breath in the air. My shoes are making the noise of a woman alone in a park, but knowing the men may be in the bushes sucking each other off makes me feel a bit safer.

There appears to be no movement in the bushes and only a couple walking their dog arm in arm with matching woolly hats on. Maybe it's too early in the night for that sort of thing.

As I turn into Sally's road I look for any signs of life near her house. A taxi might pull up with her getting out and slamming the door shut, telling Fat Neck to go back to his place tonight as she is too upset from seeing me. Or her walking slowly up the street pondering if she made the right choices and how I'd looked really good in my pink jumper. My breasts, you see, she must recall the feel of my breasts and how she lay on top holding me, making me feel as if this was the moment that would never end.

There are no lights on in Sally's house. Upon opening the gate I hear a creak which I'm not sure had been there before. The porch door opens with ease and I stand in the porch and pick up the letters which had arrived earlier that day; all for her and none for Fat Neck which is a good sign. Looking behind me first, I put the bottle of wine down on the electricity meter box and get down on my knees and pull up the carpet, which never quite fitted as Sally had cut it wonky from a spare bit her mum gave her. I hunt around underneath the carpet and feel the old brick tiles from another era. There is no key. So I pull up the carpet further as it must have slipped under. Dust flicks up into my mouth and there is no key, just floor and carpet.

Running along the back of all of these houses is an alley which the dustmen collect the rubbish from on Fridays. You have to leave your gate open so they can get in; they close it on the way out, flipping the catch down so it locks shut. There is a lot of trust here considering it's nowadays. In your day I bet you didn't have locks, just a little bolt that you twist or no bolt at all.

I shut the porch door and post the letters back through the letter box so they fall naturally into a muddle on the carpet.

Down the road I pass the familiar houses, some with their curtains open. It's only just dark and people are so busy being at home that they forget that there is an outside. Small vignettes draw me in from the street. A woman is ironing in front of the TV, a man's shirts hanging on coat hangers off the end of the ironing board. Her back is towards me. In the next house, two men are on a luxury cream sofa watching TV. One is lying flat on his back with his legs stretched out and the other has his feet curled up, his hand on the other one's foot. The next house is in darkness, and then there is the run-down house with ripped grey net curtains and flaking window frames where a TV plays to an empty room. I walk to the end of the row of houses and head down the alleyway. A cat vaults up a fence in front of me, making me jump, clawing to get to the top and balances tightrope-walker style staring back at me.

Hers is the fifth gate along. The cat has turned and jumped down the other side of the fence. I stop and swig from the bottle and put it on the ground. There is a lamp post just along the way. The orange glow shows the mess from the cats and the brambles that stretch from one house to the next, some crossing the alleyway. If I stand on the tips of my feet I can just see the back of her house, the steps that lead down to the garden from the kitchen and the back-room patio doors that open onto the crazy paving. There is a little toilet window next to the bathroom window; together they form a pair of hollow eyes. Then there is the large window belonging to the spare bedroom.

I have a kirby grip in my hair. When I had dressed for work this morning I had felt like pulling my fringe away from my face, clearing things up.

I presume I will be able to pick the lock or swing through an open window.

The wine is nearly finished so I knock back the last of it and put the empty bottle in my bag to throw away later. I push against the gate. It is locked. I look along the alley for something to stand on. There is an old armchair up the way. I drag it back to the gate and it scrapes noisily on the stones. I get a splinter in my hand as it brushes against one of the fences. There is no time for me to prise it out. The material rips from the seam on the arm when I stand on it and the chair wobbles as there is a wheel missing. Leaning over the top of the gate I can just about reach the lock and I turn it and push on the gate and it swings open. Jumping down I wedge my bag to keep the gate from swinging back shut and pull the chair back up the alley to its original position. I am sweating and wish I hadn't drunk all the wine so fast.

Her garden hasn't changed at all. Her mint is still there trying to take over the rosemary bush and camouflage the gnome in his blue hat. The shed's glass windows eye me up as I walk past.

I try the door to the kitchen; it is locked and so are the patio doors. So I take the kirby grip from my fringe and jam it into the lock on the back door. The waxy bobble on the end of it breaks off as I push it aimlessly in and out. Only car thieves and drug addicts can do this sort of thing in the films. In no time at all, my hair clip is bent and I give up poking it around. The night has got nippy and I shiver in front of the frosted-glass door to the kitchen. I pull the blow-job beret down over my ears and then I notice that the handles that should be invisible on the inside of the kitchen window are at ninety degrees, and that means the window can be pulled open if I can get my nails under the seal.

Sally must have forgotten to lock it this morning. She always opens the kitchen window as she hates the smell of toast.

They say people who are about to have a heart attack get a warning sign which is the smell of toast. It's not that useful a sign, I think, especially if you eat a lot of toast.

The window slides outwards easily and I grab the inside ledge and shift my weight off the step and my elbows are pressing down onto the outside ledge of the window. As I try to pull myself up my hands begin to slip away from the ledge, as I'm too heavy for my arms and my feet are dangling down scuffing at the wall, trying to get a grip on the bricks below. I fall to the ground, narrowly missing the drain. Looking around to check I haven't been detected by anyone, I try again, but this time I get one of Sally's plastic garden chairs from her set of four on the patio. My shoulders are now inside and I am bent over with one foot up on the ledge. I find I can lever forward and pull myself up. One foot swings in and onto the empty kitchen draining board and with an almighty heave I land one knee on top of what I find is a sieve in the sink and the other leg up on the draining board. I didn't realise I had it in me, being my size. Wine helps though, alcohol fools you into believing you can fly.

Once inside I take out my mobile to use as a torch. It casts a faint blue light to about a two-inch radius in front. It is very faint unless you have it up close.

I hold up the phone away from me, pointing the glow at the fridge. I look as if I am waiting for the fridge to talk into the phone. The picture of me has been removed but the same magnet is there holding up an article about penguin spotting in South Africa. There is also an itinerary, held up by a new magnet in the shape of a plastic carrot. My eyes are adjusting to the light. It is from an Internet travel company, the sort that Petula goes on about when she is drunk; 'the coldest way to book a holiday,' she drones.

Two nights for two people at the Royal Albion Hotel, Brighton. Breakfast included. A mucky weekend booked under her name for her and Fat Neck.

My Brighton suddenly feels invaded. How dare they go to our place.

The phone is casting a light as subtle as moonglow over the kitchen. As my eyes adjust, I can make out the tea towel hanging off the back of the stool and that there are green apples in the fruit bowl. The itinerary is in my bag. They will think it has just fallen off and disappeared and print off another one as things go missing all the time.

The enormous kitchen clock ticks and it is seven fifty-two. It was always too big for the kitchen but I never said anything. I head for the stairs and the bedroom. Walking up, the creak on the top stair unnerves me as does the dark landing with multiple-choice doors which feel as close as an itchy cardigan. The house is bigger without the lights on and more hostile since I'm not invited. My mobile light directs me across the landing to the front bedroom past the family photograph of the remaining three generations on the wall. The door is open, the bed isn't made and the street light outside is my accomplice. The duvet is a heap in the middle of the bed as if they have each flipped their side back getting out in a hurry. There are two dents in the pillows; one is heavier than the other which means it belongs to Fat Neck. He is next to the window like I was.

I go over to the bed and kneel down next to my old side. The duvet cover is new, but then again Sally said she bought a new one for every fresh relationship. This one is chocolate brown on top and fawn underneath. The sheets are fawn-coloured too. The pillowcases are brown; I suppose she chose them because of Fat Neck's saliva stains. We'd had white, all white and never a mark on them.

Bending over trying not to touch the bed in case I leave an imprint, I sniff Fat Neck's pillow. I can smell men's perfume or aftershave. It has a deep oaky smell. I get my phone close to the sheets and scan them for marks. The creases make shadows like mountainous regions, which make the bed seem a peculiar place.

I go round to Sally's side. Her pillow smells of her shampoo and her perfume, the one in the red bottle with the long neck. It is over on her chest of drawers; I used to have a squirt on my wrist without her knowing so she'd be with me all day. I get the phone and scan her side too. Nothing, it seems, but I know I have to pull the duvet right off for the hard evidence. And there it is in the middle of the fawn sheet. What I've been looking for but didn't really know until I saw it.

A dried-up sperm stain on wrinkled sheets, plus two long dark wiry pubic hairs as strong as cheesewire.

The travel-pack tissues are in my bag. I take one out and put the hairs in it and fold it into a square. There is a noise downstairs like the thud of a door and I am in that film, you know, the one where people hide in the wardrobe or behind the door or behind the shower curtain. I don't know what to do or even if the noise is from down there. Holding my breath and looking at the back of the door I wonder if and for how long the inside of her dressing gown would conceal me. My feet would stick out at the bottom though. Then I am on a windowsill in the rain, fingers clasping a brick wall, looking down at the fifty-six floors below and the yellow taxis mixing with the cars, and then I am under the bed seeing their feet walk around it, toes and more toes, muffled voices and the springs of the bed above my nose, squeaking and becoming dangerously close.

Ear-splitting silence. Must have been a car door.

I creep out of the bedroom and look over the banister down to the front door. No one is there. So I run down the stairs and through the hallway into the kitchen and let myself out through the back door. The kitchen window is shut as I found it and I can afford to let her think she has left the back door unlocked by mistake when she put out the rubbish the night before. Luckily, she has never had a good memory.

The walk back through the park is as uneventful as on the way except it is raining. I have no umbrella and the rain begins to flatten my hair and my shoes start letting in water. Not a good night for a blow job, those married men must be thinking now, too wet. They'll just stay in and chat to 'Hard and Horny from Hounslow' on the Internet, pretending to their wives in the other rooms that they're investigating the price of lawnmowers for a few hours; you hear about it all the time.

On my wrist is her perfume. It smells different, sharper. I'll wait for a while before I sniff it again as I hope it might mellow into how it used to be on her neck.

After all, nothing much seems to have changed.

13

The moon is a surprised O in the sky above Petula's head.

It is the right setting for the occasion, although it's not quite as magnificent as it could be. The full moon here is less showy than in the movies where they make it look a hundred times bigger than boys on bicycles. I am sitting on the back doorstep, the kitchen light behind me competing and winning against the moonlight. Petula says in Greece people read their newspapers by moonlight and save a lot of electricity that way. I am thinking about the moon-shaped nothingness which shoots off into the galaxy behind the moon's face and how colossal it is compared to my shadow which just about stretches to the lawn.

Petula is stood next to the flat tree stump in her garden with a small table leaning into it and the necessary objects on it: a jar of pickled onions, a hammer and a half-drunk bottle of red wine with a glass. She is wearing jeans and a T-shirt and has made me do the same, 'so what we are wearing does not deflect from the drama of the moment'.

We have already drunk a bottle and a half of red wine and I'm thinking of switching to beer.

'I think now is the time to rid myself of the cheating Welsh bastard,' she announces, clearing her throat and pulling down her T-shirt, about to make her speech which she said she wrote on the train coming back from Swansea. She unravels a small square of paper from her pocket. She raises her hand in front of her as if she is reaching out for something.

'"Wales. Spring 2005. A journey for lost love. By Petula Black.

'"After searching high and low for Ewan, through the valleys of Llanidloes, through to the hills of the Brecon Beacons, I finally caught a glimpse of someone I think was him, but still can't quite be sure, on the opposite side of the valley, holding hands with another person who could have been a woman. Through my binoculars I saw the way he looked at her with the same expression he'd given me, even though it was windy and his hair was all over his face, I guessed it was him and that my journey with one of the loves of my life was nearly at an end. So tonight on this fabulous, rain-free night and with the help from my friend ..."' She presents me to the imaginary audience, waiting until I step forward, forced into taking a bow to the flowerpot on the patio. '"... I will demolish a jar of pickled onions in front of your very eyes, symbolising ... symbolising ... symbolising that ..."' She sighs as her eyes search across the lawn for words.

'That's where I got interrupted as the man came through with the snack trolley. Now let me think.'

She picks up the hammer and starts banging it softly into the palm of her hand.

'I know. "Symbolising that ... I don't give a shit about him any more. Or his bloody poetry which I might add he never wrote about me."'

I applaud the sentiment, hoping it to be true, and she looks pleased with herself and has a swig of wine. Then she picks up the jar of pickled onions and tries to open it. Her thin hands grip the lid and she makes a straining face. She has several attempts then hands it to me.

'Can you have a go?'

I try but the lid is stuck as they always are. The tension built by Petula's speech is vanishing fast so I run into the kitchen and bang the jar on the kitchen Formica surface eight times all around the lid and then give it a go and it makes that satisfactory popping sound.

Petula has filled up her glass with red wine and has her nose in it, gulping rather than sipping. I hand her the pickled onions and she puts down the wine and says, 'Oh, music . . . Do you think I should put on some music?'

I wish she would get on with it.

'I'll put some on. What do you want on?' I say.

'Something fitting the occasion. Ah . . . The Carpenters maybe.'

We've listened to the CD non-stop since she's come home. I go back into the kitchen and push the shuffle button to give it a bit of variety.

In the garden Petula has started hammering pickled onions on the sawn flat stump while singing along. I sit back down on the kitchen step watching her aim and miss miss miss and then finally a splat. But then miss miss miss for what seems like a long time.

Initially, Petula had begun aiming at them as if she was chopping wood, lifting the hammer high in the air with both hands and throwing it down with a grunt. She was looking unnervingly like a crazed female murderer in a horror film, wild with full-moon madness. But after having left many dents in the tree trunk as the onions rolled or bounced off when she caught the edge of them, she realises that she has to hammer at them with small taps, holding the onion between two fingers like a tack.

It has become a job involving precision rather than a wild abandon, which is what she was really after. Four pickled onions crushed, most of the others on the lawn and over half left in the jar, Petula throws the hammer on the grass, picks up her wine and says, 'I should have bought the smaller jar. Come on, let's go inside. Sodding onions.'

On the kitchen table is a selection of Welsh cheeses. I have bought water biscuits for Petula, cream crackers for me and small brown loaf-shaped biscuits for the mystery guests. There is a soft blue named St Florence and a goat's cheese from Abergavenny. But my favourite is the chive and shallot one sitting underneath a strong green wax. We've bought a bottle of vintage port from the Sri Lankan corner shop to celebrate. When I bought it the man's fingerprints were left in the dust from where it had been on the top shelf and it was still warm from being up so high, near the strip lighting. The last bottle of wine I'd bought from there had turned our stomachs as it had turned to sherry. I was worried that the word vintage in his shop would mean out of date.

Petula sits down and I pour two glasses of port into wine glasses.

'You know what would go well with all this cheese,' she says.

'Those pickled onions.'

At last we both laugh and she goes to get them as I open the cheeses. It is the first moment all week that I've felt my shoulders drop and I've forgotten to think about Sally and Simon and Mum. And because I remember that I've forgotten to think about Sally and Simon and Mum that heavy feeling comes back just about where my bra digs in under my breasts.

'So how was your week?' Petula cuts a mouse's portion from the goat's cheese.

'Well. It was OK.' And I take a drop from the port.

I see Sally's face dive and the camera film fall out of the camera. The empty bar with the empty barmaid and Simon moved a little to the side in that glass box. The bird's nest and them lying on the sofa chinking glasses with their limbs interlinked and the itinerary to Brighton on the fridge illuminated by bluey-white mobile light.

'. . . very uncomfortable considering I'd paid for an upgrade and to top it all off I couldn't understand their bloody accents.' Petula takes a bite out of her water biscuit and cheese and then refills our glasses.

Petula's cheeks are pink. I make an effort to listen.

'Then you'll never guess what happened? The night I went to the Brecon Beacons National Park I arrived off the coach and went and checked into this tiny room above a pub. It was only twenty quid including a full English which, when I said to the landlord, shouldn't it be called a full Welsh since we were, you know, in Wales, he really laughed. So, well, after that me and the landlord really hit it off and he was sort of handsome like that

Welsh actor before he got so pissed, you know, ummm.' She snaps her fingers and points. 'Oliver Reed,' she says.

'I don't think he was Welsh,' I say, my eyes drifting across to the next piece of cheese.

'Well, a Welsh Oliver Reed, but you know before he drank too much and embarrassed himself on that chat show. He showed me how to change a beer barrel in the cellar and then held me so tight and lifted me off the ground when he kissed me. So I decided to stay for another night and well, oh my God! You will not believe what he did to me. I mean, I realised that Ewan was really shit in bed after being with Ivor.'

'Ivor?' I looked at the Brie with chives. The port was going down nicely.

'Yes, Ivor, just like with the engine and the dragon. But he is really tough and hung like a horse. Maybe a little too large if you get what I mean. But anyway he cured me of Ewan so you can't complain really, can you? Well, anyway, on the last night I was sat at the bar and I was watching him serve this old guy and behind him on the bar was the largest jar of pickled onions you could ever imagine and I thought to myself this is a sign and that's when this idea came to me . . . I had one of those moments when you realise something really life-changing . . . you know?'

'An epiphany,' I say.

'Mmm, though isn't that something to do with Christmas? Well, anyway, that's when it came to me, do the ritual thing. This magazine said it was part of getting rid of your past so you could be open to the future. Well, that night I was so excited after Ivor had closed up the pub, he took me from behind on the pool table and I had my first ever multiple orgasm. I was like a pig. You know they can come for five minutes at a time? Well, it just went on and on until it was a little painful.' I choked on my cheese for a moment and had a sip of my port and she continued.

'Anyway, so Ivor said he might well find an excuse to visit me in London sometime soon. I hope so as he's really, just well, ALL man. No poetry bloody nonsense sitting pretending to be something he's not. A hard-working grafter. Totally insensitive, you know, a real man. I don't know if you'd like him. He's a bit, well . . . I don't really know really, but you know what? He doesn't remind me a bit of my father. He's a bit like I expect God to look like but without a beard and more sexy and hard.'

I don't know why I wouldn't like Ivor, I never seem to get the chance to meet her secret lovers. Maybe she likes it that way, so she doesn't have to worry about what anyone else thinks.

A while later we have on Diana Ross and Petula has thankfully finished on the subject of her amazing sex with Ivor and is now drunk beyond speech. The port is finished and Petula has the tea towel she bought me on her head and is lip-syncing to the song 'Chain Reaction'. She has got me up dancing but I only have to do one to please her and then I can sit back down with the cheeses. We are drinking the vodka I hid from her initially and have retrieved from her pasta cupboard. Vodka and mango juice isn't that refreshing but it's all we've got and we're not going to the garage up the hill.

'Petula?' I ask when she sits down and has one of her cigarettes (she smokes sometimes). I have waited for the right moment, I think. 'Would you like a couple of days in Brighton next weekend?'

She smiles and I grin and hug myself as I picture us everywhere Sally will be.

14

Simon did have a girlfriend last year, you know. There is a photo of him and her and Mum and me in the Chinese down the high street. He'd just passed his A levels and Mum had booked it. She was in a good mood that night and wearing her diamond earrings. The waiter had taken the photo and it is one of those well-balanced shots with two people on each side and us all facing the camera and all smiling and nobody has their eyes closed or a red eye.

Simon had had his head shaved that week. Maybe to make wearing wigs easier, so no strands of hair fall out or maybe because he was confused about hair and what hair means. He has his arm resting on the back of Nicola's chair and she is wearing chunky jewellery in that gypsy style which was back. I guess she didn't know about him wanting to be Amanda then, as she wouldn't have been there, looking like his girlfriend. I am sat on the other side of the table with Mum and I am much bigger compared to the three of them because I am closest to the camera and also because they are thinner. Mum had asked Nicola politely about what it is that her family does and as we didn't really know her she was shy and didn't really answer until she was on her second glass of wine. Then she told us her mother used to be a bunny girl and had met her dad in a nightclub. Nicola became much more attractive to me after that.

Unlike in Indian restaurants where they play the spangly stuff, there was no music in the Chinese. This made the gaps in our conversation seem longer than they probably were. Mum had four Martini and lemonades and then told the story of how she met you after she split her skirt at a party. Mum then asked Simon how he and Nicola had met and then we sighed and giggled at the beauty of the bus-stop story and I realised I was the only one without a meeting-someone story so far and how I needed to get one.

We'd had crispy duck and pancakes as a starter. Simon was wearing a white shirt tucked into his jeans without a belt and I know now how he would have loved to have been allowed to be Amanda in that photo. When I'd brought the packet back from the chemists he'd stared at that photo and he'd commented on how contented everyone else seemed, even Mum for a change, and then he looked straight at me and said, 'You know that's not me, don't you?'

And I'd said, not realising truly what he was getting at as what he'd said was so quick and deep and my answer was more like a knee-jerk response, 'Don't be stupid, of course that's you.'

But he was right. The more I look at his eyes and his smile in that picture I can see that the smile is too wide and stretched; more false than the normal false smiles that people wear for photos, and his eyes, well, his eyes are so sad. Automatically, his smile and eyes have become the part of the photo my eyes focus on, as that's what the photo is about, not his success at his A levels. The duplicity is all there and the discrepancy lies between what he shows and what he feels. Mum would have rather he kept that smile up, you know.

And, you see, I regret it now, as when he'd said that sentence to me it was one of those moments I was supposed to talk, but didn't because my feelings didn't have the words. It's one of those conversations which could have changed everything.

15

On the table in front of me I have the tissue with Fat Neck's two pubic hairs lying open and their itinerary for Brighton. I also have a hangover from the Welsh night the night before. I have asked Petula to get a brochure on hotels in Brighton; she thinks she can get a special deal through one of her travel agent contacts. With Sellotape I stick the pubes to the top of the printout. My sunglasses take away the glare of the morning sun. I have hardly slept. The wrapper from a double pack of garlic baguettes is poking out of the pedal bin.

Four weeks today. The moon has travelled all the way around the earth since that lasagne day which was her birthday and our nine-week anniversary. The finicky light is picking up the dust on every surface. Her alarm clock should be ringing right at this moment. My elbows press down onto the breakfast bar with my head on them and I realise that twenty-eight days ago my skin last touched hers and now all that skin has become dust like on the lid of my record player. My skin will have no memory of her from now on.

On the back of the itinerary I stick the brown blank film that would have been the photos of Sally's house. I have half an hour before I go to work so I get the batteries out of the drawer and fit them back into the radio. I decide I can listen to Radio 4 as they don't play love songs.

The radio brings news of a distant war, the war they are always talking about. Three US soldiers killed in a roadside blast. A car bomb goes off in a busy street killing seventeen civilians. It seems like it's been going on forever.

I wonder if people get dumped in times of war or do they just stick it out together thinking they'll sort out the matters of the heart when all the fighting's over? Maybe 'letting someone down gently' or not is a luxury, like chocolate and stockings were. It seems all the films made about the Second World War were about falling in and out of love, dancing and wearing headscarves tied at the front and not really about the war at all. They were about being in love with the wrong person and people who went away and mostly never came back. Never about making decisions or dumping anyone or which rifle to use.

Falling in love. What strange words when you take them apart and look at them. (Even though these words aren't meant to be parted, the same as lovers.)

We know when we fall we will hurt ourselves (unless it's on a trampoline, snow or water and then there's a big splash) as we will land with a bump. But falling in love is not about gravity. It's about being suddenly in a state where you pass from being one thing to being another. Like melting ice. And when you are in the state of falling it is too beautiful to think about what might happen. Like people who jump from planes loving the act of free-fall or when that actress described her skiing accident. She skied off the side of the mountain and said that, while she rolled over and over, she was so amazed that the sky was where the earth should be and vice versa that she completely forgot about the edge of the cliff and the rocks that she was tumbling on. The upside-down sky was so incredible that the falling created a spacious time in itself. The time stretched and was like a forever when in fact it was only several seconds.

Everyone wants to fall at some point. They say 73 per cent of people think that being in love is the most important thing in the world and want to be blinded by the colours red and pink in a disco mix of passion and otherness.

They all want to find their soulmate, their match, their other half. Two halves become a couple. So I presume I am a half until I get back with Sally.

I feel less than that at the moment.

Sally said she was falling in love with me during a commercial break.

I can remember staring at a pair of white teeth on a white child on the TV and she took my hand and said, 'You know, I think I might be falling for you.' My stomach flipped, my chest flushed pink and my face went red so I knew it was true love as those are the signs you have to look out for.

We'd then kissed and she put her hand up my jumper and grabbed the flesh on my back and undid my bra with one hand. She'd then pulled down my jeans and kissed my thighs and pushed me to the point where I sobbed and she thought she'd done something wrong but it was very right.

Now that doesn't vanish overnight, does it?

16

The caff's windows are all steamed up and I am late for work.

Ten minutes before, when I should have been tying on my apron, I was standing staring at the glass box, splattered with rain, outside the police station. My brother's familiar eyes, which have been watching me walk to work from across the high street daily, have disappeared.

The MISSING picture of Simon has been removed.

The picture of the moon-faced girl is still there, but now, instead of Simon, there is a picture of a fourteen-year-old boy who looks like a drug addict. He is hunched forward in a black hooded top and has dull baggy eyes. It is a really bad photo and has been blown up so much it is blurred. It doesn't look like it was a photo of him to begin with; I reckon he just happened to be in it, to the side, accidentally like. It strikes me that he might be from a family who has never meant to take photos of him, that they don't want him remembered. At least Mum chose the best picture of Simon she felt she had, in his suit and tie; although it's not the most truthful, it shows she cared.

HAVE YOU SEEN HIM/HER/THEM?

The removed MISSING picture of Simon makes me feel like he is doubly missing.

It's clear that Simon's time in the box was up. To be fair, they all have to have their turns but I'm not feeling that fair today. Simon is my little brother and his reasons for being missing feel more important than those of the rat-like drug addict who wants no more than to be out of it. Maybe I should call Mum, to see if she's heard anything. No, I'll talk to the police first. I'm not sure if I can face her just yet.

Ruby is looking up from the counter and from her face I can tell I must look upset. Elsie is already there in her corner and she is reading Cyril's tea bag. He is bent forward trying to hear her. She is saying something about ill health from beneath her buttoned-up winter coat. We all know Cyril shouldn't be eating fried breakfasts and treacle sponge puddings.

I think I am in need of a reading. I put on my apron and stuff my coat into a carrier bag while saying sorry to Ruby for being late. She pats me on the arm and says, 'It's OK.'

'Take this over to Elsie, love,' she says, and Cyril gets up frowning as I walk over.

'Get yourself a cup of tea and sit down, love. I'm practising as I've got a table at the Psychic Fair at the town hall on Saturday.' Elsie picks up the egg sandwich that I've given her; gently her false teeth drop into the white bread. Ruby is beckoning at me from behind the counter and holds out a mug of tea for me.

'It's a two-sugar day today for you, dear. You sit down and pull yourself together. You can tell me later if you want to,' she says as she plops in two spoonfuls. Back at Elsie's table I scrape back the chair and sit down. She has egg on her lip and she licks it off. Her pink lipstick is a curve left on the bread, on the plate.

'Do you know what I watched on my video player last night?' Her magnified blue eyes are sparkling behind her glasses. I shake my head and sip the tea, which feels a bit like home.

'*The Wizard of Oz*,' Elsie says slowly as if the words are engraved with precious stones. 'I recorded it at Christmas. So gifted, that Judy Garland. They don't have the stars like they used to, do they, or the ideas. We didn't have sex then.' She sighs as she pictures herself on a bus tour of ancient Hollywood, getting to see the bathroom taps of Elizabeth Taylor.

I finish my tea and present Elsie with my mug. Elsie lifts out the bag with a spoon, slits it open with a pair of nail scissors from her handbag and tips the leaves back into the mug. She swirls them around for a while and then she sits there, frowning into the mug. According to the tea, which she says is shaped like a shoe, Elsie says I am going on a long journey and I'll need help, but at the end of it I will find what I am looking for. I realise this reading could be influenced by the storyline to *The Wizard of Oz*, but decide that Elsie must really be psychic as I am going to Brighton that weekend with Petula.

I'm going to see that Sally is OK with Fat Neck. You never know, they might be having arguments by now. Sally might be starting to notice the hairs growing out of his nose or the irritating way he eats or how he expects her to pick up his socks from off the floor. And the sex, well, the sex might have become mind-numbingly dull, like eating your favourite food of cheese-and-onion sandwiches with salt every day and then suddenly finding that they've lost their magic. Hopefully.

And then the police walk in. Elsie's eyes light up as she thinks it could be to do with her neighbourhood watch scheme, and I see Fat Neck's pubes Sellotaped to the itinerary on my breakfast bar. They could be here to arrest me. Of course I'll admit I entered without permission through the kitchen window of Sally's house and left my fingerprints on her fridge magnet and stole a spray of her scent, but my defence will be that I was trying to protect her and I didn't do anything wrong, really.

It is not our regular policeman, Geoff, who comes in for the station's bacon butties in the morning, but two officers we haven't seen before. Through the condensation on the front windows I can see a police car parked up on the pavement. They have said my name to Ruby and I turn towards them and they are looking over at me. Ruby is looking concerned and repeatedly wipes her hands on her apron.

'May we have a word, please, Miss Rodgerson?' they say as if in a scene on the TV, except they are more real, they have rain on their jackets.

'Yes,' I say, remembering it's always better to comply from the beginning.

We all move over to the empty table by the window and they sit down facing me; my back is up against the window. One has a trendy hairstyle like a man/boy from a boy band and the other's is more sensible with a side parting. Which one's going to play which part? Who is going to wear me down until I yell out the truth and they bang me up for being in love and just caring still? The trendy hair starts to speak with an accent which is from Up North.

'Now, we are here to speak to you concerning a delicate matter. Is it all right for us to speak to you here or would you prefer to go somewhere a bit more private?'

I look at his knuckles and his filed fingernails.

'No, here is fine,' I say, seeing a tape recorder on a table in a grey room.

'My name's PC Taylor and this is PC Broadbent.' The one with the sensible parting nods and smiles at me, showing his really good teeth. 'Now, it's about your brother.'

I see Simon dead in a park with a carrier bag over his head tied with a cord.

'Your mother left your work address with us as the initial point of contact should any information arise as to your brother's whereabouts, so we are here to inform you of the latest news concerning a Mr Simon Rodgerson.'

'Have you found him? Is he all right?'

He has been strangled and left in a lake, frightening the ducks.

PC Taylor continues: 'Yes, well, as far as we know he is fine. We had a phone call last week saying that he had been sighted in a local swimming baths so we have decided to close the case because when someone has been spotted they are technically no longer missing.' He pauses and sits back in his chair.

'Where? I mean, what swimming baths was it and who was it that recognised him? I mean, what did he look like?' The words come tumbling out of my mouth.

'Firstly, we cannot divulge his whereabouts as he is over eighteen and therefore deemed an adult and is therefore responsible for himself.' PC Broadbent has taken over. 'But we can tell you it was local and, well, this might be a bit difficult to hear.' He continues, his voice becoming softer, getting out and looking in his notebook. 'Last week Simon drew attention to himself and was only noticed because he came out of the changing rooms onto the edge of the pool wearing a woman's swimsuit. My notes say that it was black and that it had unnatural padding in two places.'

PC Taylor makes his hands into claws and indicates women's breasts on his police jumper. PC Broadbent shakes his head, looking across at the other officer's cupped hands, and PC Taylor drops them flat on the table.

After that he continues, 'The caller said that most people then removed their children from the pool as there was an afternoon kiddies' class on and that he was asked to leave. In fact, to give you the whole picture, the call was made by one of the staff from the pool who had called in case there was a pervert on the loose. We looked at the CCTV pictures and ran them through our picture library and matched your brother to the image.'

Simon had always loved to swim, so Amanda does too; but of course.

'We're not saying your brother is a pervert, just that the staff from the fitness centre have inadvertently found him for us and were obviously a bit concerned about a man in a woman's swimming costume being near children. I mean, he revealed himself really.'

'Will he be allowed back, to the pool, I mean? There's no law against it, is there?'

'We're not sure about that. I mean about him being allowed back. Technically he should be, but, well, what people do in their own home is fine, but in public it's a different matter of course,' he says.

'Can I see the CCTV footage?' I say.

'Sorry, no, it's property of the fitness centre,' he says.

'Where is the fitness centre?' I say.

'Sorry, it's confidential.' He looks sorry, and then it strikes me, what he said before when we had first sat down.

'My mother?' I say. 'Why would she leave me as the first contact? I mean, is she not at home?'

'Well, as far as we know she has gone away for a while and so you are our only contact now.'

Mum has gone away, at a time like this. I knew she was finding it all difficult, or at least I hoped she was as that would be a sign of caring, but to go away, now.

The police officers leave with two sausage sandwiches and I do the frying and the dishing up of food so I don't have to speak to anyone. Ruby takes the orders, serves and rings up the totals on the till. Today's special is liver, bacon and fried onions and potato with peas or carrots and Ruby makes sure that it's wiped off the board before it all runs out so that there is enough left for me.

I have Arctic Roll for my pudding, and seconds, so that I have to work the rest of the day with the button undone on my trousers, under my apron.

17

A tight white-lipped tulip painted in watercolour hangs above me on Mum's bedroom wall, exaggerating the silence in this house where there used to be plenty of action.

This is your old bedroom, with you sat on Mum's bedside table all black and white and holding a drink, in our old house. You are not a part of my memory really, you are just a series of images which belong to Mum (apart from the one I had asked for in which there is a fat toddler in a smiling man's suntanned arms who she said was you and me).

With my back to your photo, my tears plop on Mum's duvet, which is folded up perfectly without a cover on at the end of the bed, as if on a shop shelf. She used to cuddle up to me when you first went, you know? I was permitted to sleep here with her and had to try not to fidget when it got too close in case it woke her from her shallow sleep. I was able to curl up and fit into her; her knees would come up under my bottom and her arm would rest over my shoulders. I loved being there and I think she was thankful too. Simon was tiny then and would be in the cot breathing next to us.

Empty coat hangers don't do anything in her fitted wardrobe, padded with tiny bows around their silly necks. Mum has gone on a coach tour of England for all I know. She's probably bought a bargain round-the-world-in-ten-years ticket from one of those ads in the local paper.

The plants are all gone, she's thrown them out. The pots sit empty apart from a few traces of dirt at the bottom of them. Nothing needs doing, there are no everyday jobs to fill up the time in this old house of ours. Still, the phone has a tone which means she will be coming back one day and the post is neatly stacked on the kitchen surface which shows that one of the neighbours pops in from time to time. I have placed the junk mail I found in the porch on top neatly. The fridge has been turned off and the freezer has been emptied.

My adolescent posters from my room have been taken down with the Blu-tack picked off the walls leaving small damp blobs suggesting a rectangle where Marilyn Monroe used to try to hold down her skirt for me. The furniture has been moved around too and my bed is no longer under the window; it is now facing the door in the way I never liked it. Simon's room has been stripped of all its wallpaper.

I take home one of her ornaments. It is a china dog in a china basket under a china blanket. There is a bit of dust in the grooves of the blanket which sticks to my finger and I can't think where the dust could have come from since there's no one there to produce any.

18

The white plastic card in the window says 'Vacancies' from outside and 'No Vacancies' on the reverse when we get inside. Petula has a large wheelie bag and I have a small carry-all bag with a shoulder strap which keeps slipping off my shoulder. I am wearing the mackintosh raincoat and have brought a black wig in the shape of a bob and all black clothes, none with shiny buttons or zips so I do not reflect any of the seaside lights when I get to follow Sally. Petula thinks I am going through what she calls a 'French Renaissance' look. She is not aware that Sally and Fat Neck are here.

The radiator on the wall is pumping out heat and it is hard to breathe as it's so stuffy. My face is still stiff from the cold and the suffocating radiator heat is making me cough. The hallway is heavily papered and to the left there is a serving hatch which forms the window to the reception. We go and stand there and wait. There is a woman behind reception with her head lowered, her grey/black roots holding her red hair to her scalp. My body flushes and I have to take off the mac. Petula has a faint sweat on her forehead. Once the woman has pretended we aren't there sufficiently by stubbing out her gold-tipped cigarette, slurping some tea and making a phone call about bleach and bacon, she looks up at us coldly and says, 'Yes, can I help you?'

She hardly has any lips.

Petula says in her travel agent's voice, 'Yes. Hello there. My name is Petula Black and I work at the travel agent's in Dulwich. I have booked a room for two people under the name of Black?' She forces the sentence to go up at the end in an Australian kind of way.

'Black, yes, two nights. Pay in full on arrival.' And she points to a sign above the hatch which says 'Cash Only' as Petula has got her credit card in her hand. She crosses out the name in a sharp dark pencil and gets Petula to write her name and address on a slip of paper. I pass over the money I'd taken out for the weekend. We'll have to try and put things on Petula's credit card now and pay it off next month or I'll have to dip into my rent money. Above our heads other signs say:

Breakfast served 7–9am in the bar (downstairs)
All rooms must be vacated by 11am or you will be charged a fee
No pets or extra guests
No food or alcohol permitted in rooms
Licensed bar open 6–11pm (downstairs breakfast room)

The Royal Albion Hotel where Sally is staying has chandeliers and views of the old pier, but from our B&B we will probably have a view of the cars parked outside the hotel. The Royal Albion Hotel costs over two hundred pounds a night so we are in a B&B in a square on the left up from Marine Parade. It is called the Sea View, even though you have to stand outside the front to have one.

The plastic disc on the key ring says 12. The uninterested woman offers no directions but we find it on the top floor up a steep uneven staircase. I can hear the television is on in room 11 and Petula is standing rolling her eyes at the noise. A round of applause coincides with my opening the door to our room. Surprisingly, the change in temperature from the hallway makes me think I have just walked outside; it has gone from being stifling to freezing, as if a window is open. As I try to turn the knob on the radiator, Petula dumps her bag on the bed and slides open the white door to the bathroom which looks like it was once a wardrobe. In it sits a pastel-pink sink and a toilet. The wardrobe's sliding door is exactly the same as the toilet's except it is fake wood. Our room doesn't have a sea view but it does have complimentary soap. Petula is sniffing the small white packet while the tap drips.

The knob on the radiator is stuck so I check to see if the window is closed, which it is. It's one of those rickety wooden-framed windows which will rattle in the wind. The net curtain is pressed against the pane, sodden with condensation. Smearing my hand across the wet, I can see the back of another house and the bins below that belong to our B&B. We are rear-facing; you must have to pay more to get the view of the parked cars. We have two single beds the size of cots with just enough room to walk around the edges to get into them.

There are no tea-making facilities, but redeeming the bleakness there is a TV high up on a wall stand facing the beds. Petula switches it on but there is a loud buzzing noise, so she stands on the bed and swivels around the aerial on top of the set until a colourless buzzing picture appears. I can just about make out an accent from Up North.

'It's broken,' she says in a disappointed voice after having clicked through all the channels.

'I thought at least there would be a minibar,' she says, looking in the top drawer of the fake wooden chest of drawers which has a lace doily with a tasselled lamp on top of it. I agree but I won't admit it out loud as it would be like admitting that we'd paid for a dump.

'Well, that's why I brought this,' I say, opening my carry-all bag that Ruby lent me. On top of a family assortment pack of crisps and some chocolate fingers is a bottle of vodka bought from the supermarket before I left. It's their own make and since they say vodka has no taste I tell her it doesn't taste any different to the real stuff as it won't taste of anything either.

'Yes. Fantastic idea,' Petula says with her eyes lighting up, and she comes and grabs it. 'We'll need some mixers though. I know what, I'll go to that Co-op we saw round the corner and get some. We want to have a few before we go out, don't we? I can't imagine sitting downstairs with that old bitch in the bar, you would think it's Eastbourne the way she was acting. This is Brighton, where anything can happen. It's all sailors and fucking under the pier, fish and chips and cocktails.' Petula is having one of her filmic moments and I can see she is watching herself in the mirror on top of the chest of drawers.

'By the way, where are we going tonight? I haven't been down here since I was seeing that carpet seller. You remember, the one who got me that cheap underlay. I'd like to see if there are any saucy men about town; you never know who you're going to meet, do you?'

'Yes.' I mean no. 'No,' I say. 'I'll go to the Co-op, I mean.'

I want to go and see if Sally and Fat Neck have arrived yet at the Royal Albion. I need to be there when they walk into the foyer, watching from behind a newspaper or a pot plant.

'After all, you take ages to get ready and I can be done in ten minutes,' I say.

'OK. Just remember to get me some bitter lemon.' Petula takes out her mobile and checks for messages from Ivor. They were texting back and forth all the way down on the train.

I tie my hair back and loop it under the band so it'll be easy to put the wig on and put the pair of glasses which have no glass in the frames into my pocket. Petula has put down her phone, sighing, and she unzips her wheelie bag and starts to unload her make-up bag and then her toiletries and another bag that rattles as it's full of her pills. I pull on my black polo-neck jumper and mac.

'See you in a minute,' I say.

'Yeah, fine,' she says, sounding far away, as I close the door.

On my left, by the top of the stairs, is a sign on the door which says, 'Shower Room. Shut shower curtain properly or it will flood the bathroom,' and I realise I had forgotten that we didn't have a shower in the room. We'll have to share with the loud television people of number 11.

The landlady raises her head from a *Hello!* magazine as I walk past the hatch. On the back of the door is a sign saying 'Quiet! Think of our neighbours.'

I stride towards Marine Parade and I can see the lights of the new pier jutting out into the sea. It's not so new any more but I always call it the new pier because the old one is still there, and I can see the loop of the scary ride right at the end that at a certain point makes you think you are going to fall into the sea. The old pier is just about visible in the last light and has almost disappeared into the sea. In the daytime Simon and I used to sit with our anorak hoods up and watch it, waiting for it to collapse. The old pier had a glamour that the new one seems to lack, maybe because it was dying. We imagined ladies with parasols, careful not to expose their ankles to men and their skin to sunlight. It's been going away for years. A fire ruined it; there are always fires on piers, which destroy them, which is funny since they are surrounded by great amounts of water. You'd think they'd make them non-smoking or at least out of something not wooden.

I head towards the Royal Albion Hotel. I'll tell Petula I went for a breath of fresh air and a bag of chips as I'll be noticeably longer than the Co-op run would take.

The sky is so panoramic here it's as if I am looking through a wide-angled lens. I can see the last warmth of the sunset to my right and to my left where the night has already begun the sea has merged with the inky sky. That is why people with big egos like Fat Neck should live by the sea, so they can remember how little they are.

The Royal Albion has a strip of carpet on the pavement to welcome you in, as if the idea of comfort starts somewhere just outside the hotel. I marvel at how they keep it so clean with so many footprints. A man opens the door for me and I'm not ready as I haven't put on my disguise yet but feel I have to enter as he's holding open the door, waiting.

I'm worried that I'll walk straight into them.

The reception area to the hotel is large and richly carpeted. My eyes flick around, checking for Sally and Fat Neck. There is no sign of them. In the centre there is a round brushed suede seat and a chandelier hanging down above it. It looks like the *Titanic*. To the right is a curved staircase with a white pillar in the middle. I can smell the food roasting in the kitchen and hear the chinking of Martinis and quiet conversation from the bar. I pull the belt of my mac tighter until it digs into my flesh and then find I can't breathe so I loosen it again. There appear to be no pot plants to hide behind and I am without a newspaper. The lobby of a hotel should be much busier than this and I am worried that I'm too exposed. I see a sign in fancy writing pointing to the ladies' toilets and go in there for a moment so I can put my glasses on and adopt my disguise. There is expensive hand soap in a gold oyster shell and hand cream in bottles that you can remove and put back and light bulbs all around the mirror which reminds me of the suicidal show tune 'Send in the Clowns'. I wash my hands and then squirt loads of the cream on them and then excitedly cover my arms and face with it, because it is free. I have dispensed too much so it's ended up sitting on the top of my skin and I have to wipe it off with tissues, which are held in a gold jewelled box which covers its cardboard one. It smells buttery and I wish I hadn't gone so mad with it as it's making me feel a little sick. I wipe my hands with a luxurious hand towel from the neat, folded pile.

Standing back, the glasses really do suit me, I think, but I wish they had lenses in them for total authenticity. They give me the air of a secretary about to take notes who isn't so junior that she has to make the coffee all the time. She has responsibilities. I pull the wig down on my head, tucking my hair into the back of it. The wig sticks out at the bottom where I hoped it would curl under after I gave it a trim. It was one of Elsie's and smells of digestive biscuits and old hair inside where the netting is. Standing back looking at my reflection, I take pleasure in not looking like me. The dark hair seems to bring out a severity in my face that is not usually there and the glasses intellectualise me immediately. People will think I am clever and maybe a little French. I didn't bring the blow-job beret as that would be just too caricatured and probably end up drawing attention to myself rather than allowing me to merge into the background of the hotel.

I stand looking past my image and for a while let my eyes go out of focus. This is the tricky bit. How do I know where Sally is going to be now she's away from her routine? I will have to try and link myself psychically with them. Closing my eyes, I concentrate on seeing an image that might help me as to their whereabouts. A bagel filled with cream cheese pops into my mind, which is of no use at all. Now, Sally wouldn't have been able to get time off work on a Friday so they would have come down on the train from Victoria after six. It's seven twenty-two now on my mobile. That means they might only just be arriving now.

What do they do in the films again when they are detecting? They phone the room or even better they find out the room number by looking over the counter while they get the receptionist to go on a false errand. They creep along a window ledge from another room and look in the window. They pop into the room behind the chambermaid and hide behind the door until she has put clean towels in the bathroom and left, pulling the door shut, revealing the detective. They hide in the wardrobe, under the bed, plant bugs in the plants, have binoculars, pretend to be window cleaners on one of those swinging pulley things.

Everything is too confidential nowadays. I'll never find out what room they are in especially if they have used a coded dirty-weekend married name. But that was in the days when sex before marriage was disgusting, so if they did that it would only be in a tongue-in-cheek way. The room will almost certainly be under Fat Neck's name as he's probably the really controlling type. No, hold on, I have the itinerary in my pocket. Two nights' accommodation booked by Miss Sally Hunter.

There is a book of matches in the ashtray, folded back in such a way so it exposes its teeth. The phone number here is printed on the front under the majestic swirly emblem of the Royal Albion Hotel. I take out my mobile and call the number. They answer almost immediately and I wonder where the woman who has answered it is, whether she's in a special room with a headset on.

'Good evening. The Royal Albion Hotel?'

'Hello. Can I speak to Sally Hunter, please?'

'Is that Hunter with an H?'

'Yes,' I say in a voice like a newsreader's.

'Hold on. Putting you through.' She speaks like a newsreader too.

And the phone clicks and starts ringing and I can see a white phone on a bedside table with buttons for room service and bell-boys all over it and I hang up.

I haven't heard her voice since I left and the thought of her speaking to me as if I'm a stranger or hotel staff makes me turn cold. I'm not sure what I'm doing, but I know I still want her to want me, for me to be her number one, her Top of the Pops, and that I don't want to reveal too much at the moment.

The matchbook is now in my pocket with the itinerary which still has Fat Neck's pubes attached with Sellotape and the brown film. I crack open the door and peer out into the foyer. A party of six are over by the desk checking in. Two blonde women with long black coats holding glittery handbags are waiting by the brass revolving doors. A man stands alone checking his mobile phone.

The bar is to my right as I walk out. The doors are closed and they have small squares of glass in the upper part. I go up to the door and try to see through one of the squares. The glass is thick and ridged and I can only make out that the bar looks quite busy and everyone is distorted. After only a moment of me not being able to see, a man is behind me saying excuse me please. I turn slightly round and walk straight into his chest. I can smell his after-shave and I can tell he has just showered. He says sorry and I don't look up but know it's Fat Neck from the smell and before I know it he has brushed past me and entered the bar and I can see Sally waving at him in a low-cut dress and her hair is up revealing her cheekbones. He strides towards her and then sits down, placing a camera on the table, and the door has shut and the squares are like thick lenses in someone else's glasses disabling my vision.

She looked excited and alive. Not so long ago she'd looked at my Turkish bread and olives like that and I realise that she must be fickle. Her heart is inconsistent and if it is that changeable then surely she will be able to switch it back to me again? All I have to do is remind her that she loves me and not him.

Now, in the films, the character playing me would decide they have to sleep with Fat Neck or hire a prostitute and take photos to reveal to Sally that he can't be trusted and is a man like any other man, thus causing her to return to me with a great remorse for how she's been acting. But the thought of what lies beneath his trousers makes me feel uncomfortable so I decide against that plot.

Maybe I could be seen with a new love and make her jealous and then when she realises that jealousy is a feeling which really equates to love she will have a good hard think about it, maybe in a park, by a lake (with music playing in her head), and have a wonderful realisation that it's me me me she wants. Yes, it'll be hard to let him down, but best in the long run, I'll say.

Thinking like Sally and Fat Neck, I walk towards the reception desk and ask the receptionist for a recommendation for a restaurant, as if I wanted an intimate night's dining near there. The Carpenters are playing. It's the song 'Close to You' and I can't believe the coincidence as the words are so apt. She glances at me and then immediately down in front of her at the stapler and hardly appears to detect my disguise as she writes down two of the guests' favourite places on a piece of paper with the same majestic swirl as the matchbook has on it. As she hands me the piece of paper her eyes seem to rest nervously on my outstretched hand and I feel she must be embarrassed by my bookish looks. It must be ever so good, my disguise.

Just knowing where Sally might be going makes me feel a surge of optimism and I decide I must rush back now via the Co-op to get ready to go out. We could be down in the bar opposite the pier in twenty minutes, where I figured I should be able to see the entrance to the hotel in time to see them leave. But that is assuming they are going out for dinner and not having room service and eating it off of each other's genitals.

19

By the time I have got back to the B&B with a bottle of bitter lemon and a can of lemonade Petula is sitting on the end of the bed, ready. She has straightened her hair with tongs and has on silvery-blue eyeshadow and an opaque lip gloss.

'Where have you been?' Her eyebrows are pencilled into an inquisitive curve.

I am out of my disguise and out of breath, sweating under my mac as I walked back as fast as I could. I shall have to have a flannel wash with my hands in the sink as there is no flannel.

'I went for some fresh air and chips and well . . . all these memories came back and I started to think about how we used to come on holiday here and those lovely bags of chips. Do you think Simon might have come back to find a sort of . . .'

'Oh well, best not to dwell on the past, eh? Never does any good, does it?'

Petula stands up looking uneasy, as if our weekend could be spoilt by me starting to talk about 'my everlasting problems' as she calls them. She is never quite comfortable with a subject if it doesn't include her.

'Now let's get a drink inside of us so we can go and hit the town. You get ready while I pour us a couple of strong ones.'

She removes the clear plastic bags from the two small plastic glasses from the sink with the soap, and then fills them half full with vodka and then our mixers. I change into my going-out bra, the one which holds me together, and put on a scooped black top and my black hide-it-all trousers. I have black leather boots that

I found in the charity shop which needed resoling on the heel. I put on some mascara and red lipstick.

'You know, you look quite nice tonight,' Petula comments. 'It's about time you got out there again.' Then she sighs. 'While you were out I got thinking about Ivor. Do you think I was just using him for sex? I mean, it was all great when I was there but now I am here I can't seem to remember what he looks like, his face has gone missing. I just keep thinking about all the fun we had, you know, in the sex department. When I think of him I just get flashes of him on top of me, pressing me into the crates of small tonic waters in the cellar or me on top of the bar being lifted down onto him.'

I look in the small square mirror on the bathroom cupboard and decide I might try my winking again tonight as I have combined it now with a smile which gives it an added extra, like a bonus.

Petula has on a gold sequinned top with strings at the back which hold it on and a pair of shiny black trousers. Her shoulder bones stick out like shiny nodules. She has tied a glittery black scarf around her neck and looks like she is in a music video.

'You only saw him for two nights, remember?' I say. Then as if by magic a text message comes through and Petula reads it and laughs a little vividly.

'Listen to this,' she says picking up a glass and holding it towards me with her mobile in her other hand.

'It's from Ivor. He's said "Hello Pet" (that's what he calls me now) "I've been thinking about you all day. It's made my Welsh breakfast sausage go so hard I don't know if I'll be able to have the pub quiz later." Aw . . .' she says, looking up. 'Isn't he just so romantic and sexy?' And then her face does that look that people do on TV when they've had an idea with a binging noise. 'What if he's the one though? God, can I see myself as a landlady of a pub in the middle of bloody nowhere serving cheese on toast to a group of middle-aged farmers? But I mean he could be the one, couldn't he? God knows, anyone could be the one. Thank goodness Ewan went when he did, as I thought he was the one at one time and I didn't know that he wasn't then, did I?'

I drink my drink down straight and Petula glances across and does the same.

'One more?' she says.

'No, we'll decant it into the bottles and drink it down the road.' I say, getting my mac back on as we should go now. Petula empties out half the bitter lemon and lemonade into the sink and then carefully pours the vodka into the bottle and can.

'Are you taking your mobile?' Petula asks.

'No, I don't think so, in case I lose it,' I say picking up the key and sliding some loose change into my pocket along with my bank card. I will have to get some money out from somewhere.

Petula looks at me and then at her phone, not sure whether she can leave it alone. Then she takes a semi-deep breath, presses a button on the top of the phone hard until it bleeps and puts it on top of the chest of drawers.

'You're right. It'll do Ivor good to think I'm ignoring him.' She pulls on her padded jacket with a fur trim around the hood.

As we go to leave the B&B the woman shouts out the word 'key' at us as we walk past the hatch. She points to a sign on the wall behind her which we must have missed.

No keys to be taken off the premises.
Ring the bell after 11pm for the night porter.

She looks us both coolly up and down as we hand over the key and Petula says thank you a little too loudly to make a point. As we walk towards the sea, Petula links her arm in mine. She is pulling me closer to her in that way which says it's really cold out, isn't it, but without saying it. It always surprises me when she does that, one of her rare sudden displays of affection, and so in return I squeeze her hand silently until people come towards us and then I let go.

From the outside we look like any two girls out for a Friday night in Brighton. The bar we go into is round the corner from the Aquarium and you can just about see the entrance to the Royal Albion if you take a seat near the door. From outside the bar smells of stale alcohol and thinks it will pull the crowds in with an all-night happy-hour drinks offer. It is empty apart from a group of lads on a stag do, standing at the oval bar, who are trying to attract our attention by being really loud and staring at us over their pints as they hold them to their lips. They say that men lift their drinks up to their mouths and women dip their heads down to their drinks, which makes women sound like they are horses and have no hands. Petula is pretending she hasn't noticed that the stag party are looking at her, even though she keeps throwing her hair around; it's not making it easy to concentrate on the entrance to the Royal Albion. There's been nothing yet, just a few taxis starting and stopping.

There are loutish shouts at the bar as the head stag gulps down a pint, letting it spill down the front of his shirt. The other men cheer and order the same again and whatever you're having, love, to the barmaid loudly. Meanwhile a hen party has traipsed in. Each of them is wearing bunny ears and the bride-to-be has a learning to drive sign on her back and a veil tucked under a tiara. They are in short skirts and high heels. The stags applaud and whistle as the girls go and stand around the other side of the bar with tight looks on their faces.

Across the way people come and go from the Royal Albion. As it's still relatively early, most of the rooms above are lit, some with their curtains open. A man with a towel around his waist stands at the window scratching his groin area, and I can't tell if he is watching us or just looking out aimlessly. For every hotel across the land there must always be a man in a towel scratching his balls standing by a window, I've seen it before from train windows and minicabs. Petula takes out a cigarette.

'This bar is shit,' she says, flicking her lighter. I agree, it doesn't seem to have any ambience.

'I didn't come to Brighton to stare out to bloody sea, you know, and those men are annoying me, so bloody juvenile. They just think they are such big men.' She lights up, not yet drunk. It's early for her to be smoking.

'OK,' I say, shifting in my chair. It's been a while and Sally and Fat Neck could have already left or gone back up to the room while I was walking back to the Sea View. This bar was a bad idea; there are too many possibilities in Brighton and I wish Petula wasn't with me. I should have come alone. She'll be wanting to go to bars I don't want to go to and I'll have to go otherwise she'll have one of her dramatic strops.

'Where do you want to go next?' I ask, trying to sound enthusiastic, as getting Petula out of one of her moods means either letting her get drunk to the point where she can't speak, or flattering her endlessly. But then, out of the corner of my eye, I think I see Sally's hair getting into a taxi and I am annoyed now as I took my eyes off the hotel only for a moment.

The taxi drives off and they are gone (if they were ever there).

'Let's go to that pub where they have all those drag queens. I can't be bothered with men at the moment. I'd rather be in a gay bar than go out with all those pissed blokes looking for their last shag before they marry their poor unsuspecting fiancées. I mean, look at them, they behave as if they've never been allowed to have a drink before. At least with Ivor I know I'm the only one he's got, even if it's only for sex . . . I mean, he said it's not often that he got attractive female travellers staying in the local vicinity and all the local women were either married or had two heads.'

Petula necks her pink cocktail and grimaces. The hen party are starting to liven up and there is a scream as one of the girls stirs her drink with a red vibrator then sucks it. The other girls clap and the stag party look on defeated as if it's a competition to see who can have the most outrageous time.

'Euch, cranberry juice,' says Petula. 'Come on, it's only up the road, isn't it?'

We leave and the chilly sea wind smarts our eyes. It lifts up Petula's hair at the back and presses us along the front, sweeping us slightly off the ground. We swig from Petula's bitter lemon and vodka which she'd hidden in her bag and I am trying not to appear to look at the Royal Albion. Instead, I focus on the pebbles on the beach and stay out of the cycle lane which is just a line drawn on the pavement. I point out to Petula that a blind person wouldn't know it was there, and wonder if their dogs are taught to look out for such things. Petula says maybe in Amsterdam the dogs know about the lanes, as they are ahead of their time there and have sex hotels and ways of dispersing gangs of youths from hanging around and intimidating people by playing organ music really loudly at them through tannoys.

As we pass the fish and chip shop it makes me think of sausages in batter and my stomach grumbles and I realise I haven't eaten since the mid-afternoon packed lunch on the train, but I can't divert us now as I've already lied and said I've had a bag of chips.

'You know this is a gay bar?' the bouncer in a black padded jacket says to us, putting his arm across the door as we go to walk in. Petula says *yes* in a know-it-all voice and I smile at him apologetically with a look that tries to make him realise that, yes, I am in love with a woman so that should give me a rainbow-coloured freedom pass to enter this pub. He lets us in anyway, he has to really due to the new anti-discriminatory European rules which say that anyone is allowed to go into any bar regardless of who they are.

Inside, the pub is filling up by the bar. I can see there are empty tables at the back near the pool table. It is mostly men in tight T-shirts and jeans who want to stand up and be the first to be seen. There is a difference between those who sit down and those who stand up in bars and it's not just about if there are any seats free. Women like to sit down, as do gay couples that have been together for twenty years.

I am a sitter if I can be, but Petula isn't. That's probably why

Petula has a tiny bottom and mine spreads onto other people's seats on trains.

At the end of the bar there is a fed-up drag queen in a wide backcombed black wig sat on a stool, smoking, with two clear drinks with ice and lemon in front of him which is probably gin. A strapless blue sequinned dress with a split up the side cuts him under the arms and wasted flesh hanging off his shoulders drops over the edges. From his face and legs you would think he was younger, but his chest is wrinkly and neck ringed with age. He has a medium-sized cleavage pushed together and covered in glitter and his legs are perfectly shaped and smooth in light-coloured tan tights.

Men have better-shaped women's legs than women do.

The make-up is immaculate. I go and stand next to Petula at the bar and look. He has highlighted over his eyes on the bone that's under his eyebrows with a silvery blue like Petula's and then gradually darkened into the sockets. He has powdered his nose and chin to make them softer and tried to disguise his Adam's apple with foundation and more powder. There are long lines of rouge on his cheeks to suggest cheekbones. His lips are painted on and outlined, bigger than what's probably underneath, and he has long false eyelashes which look as if they are heavy to lift, either that or it is his bored demeanour. I am drawn to his red glossy lips and his painted red finger-nails as he sips his drink. His hands seem large and bulky compared to the glass.

He is performing tonight. There is a showbiz photo of him on the door, a professional black-and-white one with his head thrown back, laughing.

The DJ is setting up behind the decks and starts to play Kylie. Petula has a ten-pound note in her hand and is ordering two Slippery Nipples.

I sit down at a table at the rear of the bar while I wait for Petula to get served. Two women with short spiky hair are playing on the pool table. They have roundish faces and no make-up on. They have tiny breasts under their polo shirts and I wonder if on a certain day at a certain point they gave up on wearing skirts and relaxed into looking that boyish. I don't know if they ever wanted to look like women (as women are told to) and then I think about whether it's to do with want at all.

And what is a woman if Simon thinks he is one deep down?

The drag queen at the bar is called a female impersonator but there is nothing particularly female about him looking like that. Most women don't want to look that glamorous any more as people would say they look like drag queens. It's all become a bit unclear. There's nothing particularly female about the pool players either. And I am only called feminine because I have long hair and wear lipstick and am fat and curvy with breasts too big for my bra, but female and feminine are separate things, and yet they're not, not really.

And then it becomes quite clear, Simon has been a male impersonator all his life, he has had to pretend to the world that he is a boy when really inside he's been a girl. But why would he want to be a girl when being female is about artifice, let's pretend, putting things on, in, pulling bits off, plucking, waxing, cutting; squeezing into a shape or an idea.

The drag queen knows it's not about looking natural, with his caked-on face and breasts made from the fat on his back. Maybe the androgynous pool players have got it right.

I wonder if Sally feels more like a woman because she is with Fat Neck.

Thank God Petula is back. She was laughing with the barman, safely flirting with him over the names of our drinks, and I marvel at how easily she makes friends.

Before I know it I am feeling a little slurred, my debit card is behind the bar and we are on doubles. I have been squished into the corner by a group of foreign students who have taken over our table. Petula has been chatting to the bouncer for twenty minutes so I decide to go to the loo and I am in a queue for the Ladies behind two men. Madonna is playing upstairs, 'Like a Virgin'. I am nearly at the front of the queue and the two men go into the cubicle together. I feel like saying something but remember the new equality law and think maybe it extends to the toilets. After several minutes I am trying not to jig up and down outside when they reappear and I wonder what they have been doing. There is piss all over the floor and the toilet seat. I hover over the seat and have to hold on to the empty toilet-roll dispenser to steady myself as I am more drunk than I thought.

Edging my way through the dancing crowds back to our table, I can see Petula leaning against the wall by the entrance, talking and blowing smoke out with the bouncer. When I get back, the foreign bunch has spread out over our seats. I say excuse me and push back into my corner. One of the girls has dark elfish hair and is looking at me from across the table. She isn't bad-looking so I put my head down and look up with one of my eyes slowly winking and lips semi-parted in a sultry smile I have practised. She looks away and I feel foolish. She gets up and walks over to the pool table with her back to me and I strain my head to look for Petula. The winking doesn't work this time but I tell myself that it can't have a one hundred per cent success rate or everyone would be doing it.

The foreign students up and leave after the one drink that they made last for over fifteen songs. My table seems to be the only empty space for a while and I tear up a drinks mat advertising cider. I am relieved when three women arrive and then fill the space after asking if the seats are free. Two are clearly a couple and have started kissing energetically in front of me and I can see their tongues in each other's mouths going round and round like a washing machine. The girl with them has sat down next to me, opposite them, and is concentrating on rolling a cigarette. She looks as if she has had to get used to her friends doing this and wants to avoid watching it. She is young, like a student, and I glance at her hands and then a drink arrives on the table from the barman and Petula is waving at me from near the door, gesturing that she is going back outside. I watch her go back to the entrance and she points at me from outside and the bouncer and she both wave at me. Once hard, his face is now overly animated and friendly. Petula has a straw in her drink and as she slumps back against the wall I can see she is sucking it for the bouncer in such a way that made Ivor and Ewan undress her very quickly before.

The arrival of the drink is a good thing as it's made me seem popular and like a local. My finger taps on the glass to the music that has crept increasingly louder since we arrived. You're not supposed to realise it, like the adverts which are slightly louder than the programmes on the TV. It is becoming very hot in the corner and so I undo my mac and take my arms out of it, trying not to nudge against the student girl next to me.

Then the main lights go off and I want to make a joke to the girl next to me about murder in the dark but I don't. The stage lights come up and there is a fake drum roll and people hush and form an audience around the stage and I am thankful to be pulled out of myself by the entrance of the drag queen.

20

Candyfloss floats on top of the dark urine, a delicious cocktail shot called Brighton Pier.

I never realised the pier had such an underbelly.

'I'm going for some fresh air,' I'd said to Petula, holding onto the handrail outside the bar.

The Aquarium is closed for the night; the fish have all retired, sleeping in their unblinking manner and that famous stingray named Ray, who you can actually touch and who smiles and waves in a weird celebrity way, knows he can stop performing and just float.

All things change when the light has disappeared. The moon grants permission for things unimaginable by day. I've heard that some people can only have sex with the light off or at night. And some people demand that you keep the light on. Some people are freed by the dark and others are trapped in it.

There is safety in light. Elsie sits behind her lounge window with the orange neighbourhood watch sticker on it each night, in her high-back chair with just the lamp and the kitchen strip light on for comfort. The sun setting marks the start of her curfew and she doesn't go out after dark. She sits and waits for the burglars and the rapists and the paedophiles with her theatre binoculars in her lap, her phone a hand span away on her telephone table. She sits by her window when there is nothing else for her to do. It fills the time between having her tea, going to bed and watching what she calls her programmes. I think of her as a balding Miss Marple, watching and noting down the details of the street outside on her notepad with the pencil neatly tucked into the spiral at the top when not in use. She saw a three-legged fox once at ten to nine. She showed me the pad the next morning as evidence, as if writing it down on the pad made it true. Her handwriting is like yours used to be, a bit spindly.

And some people like Petula use the light. She told me she only really enjoys sex with the light on so she can see the other person's sex face. She likes to see the contortion, she says it turns her on to know what she can do to someone else. I kept my eyes shut with Sally; whether the light was on or off I kept my eyes closed as I liked the shapes on the inside of my eyelids that Sally's hands used to make when she touched me.

But now I can see under the pier the small orange glows of fire from drug addicts burning things on foil, and other people lurking around in the shadows around the iron pillars. There are dogs too. I want to go and see, I don't know why but maybe it's for the same reason that Simon and I once went to Cardboard City in Waterloo on an outing. To see something that was as far away as possible from Mum chopping the tops off of our boiled eggs with that frustrated expression, something that would shock us into realising how lucky we really were. It didn't change a thing.

You know, they cleared away all the cardboard shacks, along with the homeless people, and made it into a huge round cinema that no one I know goes to, and, by building what is called a state-of-the-art cinema, it has made the homeless people totally homeless. I'm sure people go now without even knowing what was once underneath.

Funny how we weren't allowed out after dark in those days, but I am now. Of course I was a child then and vulnerable, but am I that different? I still have the same feet. Though we were allowed out at night when we were away at the holiday camp, that was only to go to the clubhouse where bands with names like the Las Vegas Sisters and Pink Blancmange would come and entertain us. We would dance until our fringes were stuck to our faces with sweat and we had stitches in our ribs and Mum would stay in the caravan with one of her love books and a Martini and lemonade, no ice. Simon and I were told to stay together and never leave one another and we did what we were told as we got on, mostly, which I know is a rare thing between siblings. We knew we had to stick together, and Simon was no trouble at all.

By daytime, I know this area as the bit of the beach where the toilets are with those swirly wet sandy floors, which you hope is the water from wet feet and not children's wee. But stood here, by night, watching the waves froth onto the pebbles and the light from the pier fall just past me, it is all so unfamiliar, I am un- familiar. And I realise this beach isn't for night-time, the night- time beaches are the ones where a coconut could knock you out at any time.

Before coming down the steps to the beach, I bought six hot doughnuts from the American Donuts stall on the pier. They are covered in sugar and slightly damp and underdone on the inside, hot and crispy to the bite. The grease has come through the brown paper bag making it slightly transparent and my hand is all oily like from when you get a sausage in batter from the fish shop in a perforated-edged envelope. I bought six as it's more economical and I am eating them all as quick as I can as they won't be any good once they've gone cold.

Above me I can hear the dull thud of the music from the pier. My boots are next to my feet with the socks tucked inside and my feet are crunching back and forth on the pebbles and I know I'm hurting my soles into trying to feel as if I am real. The sea hurts my toes as it comes and goes along with the sensation in my feet, staining the bottom of my trousers a few shades darker black. The sea sounds as if it's rolling its tongue across the pebbles, throwing itself crossly forward then dragging itself back like a heavy curtain. The motion is mesmerising and I stay stuck for a while until a dog snarls under the pier.

Looking back, I wonder what type of music if played on a tannoy would move the gang from under the pissy-smelling pier; maybe

Rod Stewart's song 'Sailing' over and over again would drive them up the steps into rehab. It's never really crossed my mind until now, but even though I know they are drug addicts and have a reputation for stealing what they can from their mothers' purses, maybe they are quite happy as they are, as they don't really know the full extent of their unhappiness. Or perhaps they are oblivious to how happy they might be and how small pleasures are to be found in making a packed lunch for someone to take to work, like I did for Sally. Maybe they are lost like Simon and don't want to be found and don't know what else to do as the drugs must make you feel like you don't have any choice.

It's turned cold now and this is nothing like it was before; this place and the drug addicts are menacing as they walk out from under the pier. I turn away and pull on my boots, catching the skin of my right leg in the zip as I rush to leave. Then I look up to the pier and wave at the red square which could be a lifebuoy or a meeting point, pretending it is someone peering down waiting for me. They are getting closer, the druggies, so I shout out up at the pier, 'You stay there, I'm just coming.' And in my mind the person on the pier does a thumbs-up sign and I feel safer already. The gang stops at the wall which divides the pebbles from the path and I have to make my way past them up the steps to the promenade. My back flinches knowing they are behind me. I almost expect to be hit over the head with a bottle, but nothing happens. I go onto the pier as if I am really going to meet up with a friend, and I realise I have convinced myself that there is someone on the pier waiting for me and that they must just be around the back of the palmistry hut where I always wanted my hand read as a child. Now it's empty, I suppose as it's out of season. I can't tell from up here whether the gang are girls or boys because their hoods are glued up around their heads. But I guess they are mostly boys, as they are sitting with their legs open and are flat-chested.

No one is waiting for me.

Past where you can have your name written on a grain of sand

and just before the entrance to the fruit-machine hall, there is a group of four men with ruddy faces poking their heads through the same holes which Simon and me did all those years ago. They think it is funniest to be the mermaid and are taking turns having their photos taken on mobile phones. The two painted characters, the mermaid and the diver, are sat on a rock which looks like the surface of the moon and the mermaid is brushing her hair and holding a hand mirror. The men are pulling the sort of faces which they assume a mermaid would have, their lips shaped in an ooh and their eyes stretched open. The painted figures are surrounded by a tropical-looking sea and Brighton Pier is featured in the background. You can tell it's Brighton Pier because they've included the helter-skelter in the middle and also because no one would be daft enough to paint any other pier on a painting to be featured on Brighton Pier.

Inside the fruit-machine hall, I go up to the change counter. The sign above it is illuminated red around the edge and they have written the word 'change' in a Western-film-type lettering. The girl is sat piling up coins into slots on a wooden tray and she doesn't look like she is from a Western. I ask for a pound's worth of ten-pence pieces and watch her pick up the pile of coins and drop them into the brass dish between us, without looking up. Behind her there are shelves of stuffed toys, presumably given by people who didn't really want them after they'd won them. I play on a fruit machine called Golden Fruit. I win 20p when three cherries appear and the machine lights up and I'm not sure whether to gamble it all. I do and lose. But for that small moment I think I'm going to hit the jackpot and my stomach flips. That's what keeps you playing.

Later, leaving after I've spent another pound on the horse race where the miniature plastic horses mounted by their tiny jockeys run their cranky race over and over again, I see the girls from the hen party with their heads poking through the seascape. They are staggering about, bare-legged and with drunken arms around each other's shoulders.

Revisiting memories is such a bad idea. I realise that there is nothing physically here in Brighton any more, it's all in my mind and I don't know how much of it is true without the photographic evidence to prove it, without the writing on the pad. I wish my memory would allow me back in so I could live back there for just a little while, when it was simply me and Simon and Mum. But nothing is working for me here. The drug addicts are trying to get out of it, whereas I'm trying to get back into it.

Instead, I'll go back to the bar to see if I can get that girl smoking roll-ups to talk to me. She should as she is minding my drink and coat and I shall buy her a drink as a thank-you reward.

21

The seagulls are crying frantically as I wake up at the Sea View. These days I never seem to remember going to sleep.

My trousers are all twisted round and I am fully clothed and alone on top of one of the beds and feeling incredibly cold and sick. Even lifting my head is an effort.

Once, I mean last night, I remember there was a road that led to a party and I was chatty and quite the entertainer in front of the student, Kate, and I wish that that journey could be the whole story as after that there is just a blank space surrounded by an irksome feeling that I did or said something wrong.

Petula's bed is empty and untouched and the room is as we left it before we went out. Her tongs are still plugged into the wall, her make-up bag is gaping open like a fish mouth and her phone is on the chest of drawers. The room is as cold as we left it. I check in my trouser pocket for my debit card and all there is is a scrap of paper with Kate's number on it. It is on lined paper like out of a child's schoolbook and she has underlined the number twice. There is a seven in her phone number and she has crossed it like the French do. Her handwriting looks older than she does. She has a shaggy hairstyle like a pop star and said something about being Kylie's number-one fan. I remember watching her mouth the words to one of her songs in the bar. I've never had someone else's number in my pocket before, either on a piece of paper or a business card, like they hand over a lot in American films.

My mac is on the floor next to the bed and I look in the pockets for my debit card and there it is wrapped up in Sally's itinerary with my glasses frames and the matchbook. And I hear that famous morning-after line, 'I didn't, did I?' I recall the maroon carpet of the Royal Albion's reception when I went looking for her there after the party and stumbled around in the lobby until I was slung out with a harsh hand pulling at my coat sleeve as I called the concierge 'a prize tosser'.

My stomach clenches and I rush to the toilet in the wardrobe and I am sick into the bowl. It's all black and bitty and tastes a bit of meaty aniseed. There are tears on my cheeks and I long for the hand that holds up the hair or rubs the back at times like these. After nothing more comes up when I retch, I peel off my trousers and release my bra and climb under the sheets, deciding not to move until my stomach settles. My mobile reads 11.37 and there are no messages as usual. I have missed the free breakfast but wouldn't have wanted it now anyway.

Petula must be with the bouncer, her bed is as she left it.

My hands go to my stomach and it feels strange, like it's a bit hard, a little balloon-like. Normally it wobbles when I grab the fat and shake it around a little, but not now, it seems swollen and solid. My fingers feel blown up too and it's as if I am containing something other, an otherness.

My eyes close and the room becomes a bobbing hospital, the bed a cartoon boat; the ceiling peels back as if it is a lid on a sardine tin, revealing the sky and the sky is just the sky. The sun is a greasy fried egg from the morning breakfast I missed and there are no words to describe how I feel. My mouth twitches and my brain has no fresh ideas apart from these and I feel nothing.

Is nothing a feeling or just an absence of feeling?

Whatever. But in this case I think I shall just sleep. My arm cups my belly and I wait for the comfort of absence that only sleep or extreme drunkenness brings.

22

As the day fragments into dusk, I've woken up to myself. The molecules in the air are shimmying up and down and I've woken up to myself. But not in the conventional sense like when I realise I've been behaving selfishly and not putting myself enough in other people's shoes.

I have woken up looking at myself.

My arm is over the sheet and the sheet is under a bally mustard blanket and I prod at the fat to wake myself up. After no reaction, I grab the skin on the back of my arm with my see-through fingers and pinch it. No response, so I stroke my arm and find the skin is rough with dry bobbly bits, which I'd go and loofah off if I wasn't so out of myself. But saying I touched myself as if I am a separate entity would be pushing the truth a little as I have only a vague sense of my hand, which is loosely transparent and hardly visible when I look at it, but I can sense it's there all right. Across from me my real eyes are closed tight, I'm not having any of it, it seems. The other me is on my side, as if I am on a vague notion of a beach towel, back from a swim, with my head resting on my outstretched arm. I am looking down at the long landscape which is my body wrapped in the sheet, like I've been washed up. I tug down the sheet and the blanket to have a good look.

There are two nearly straight lines on my body which I would draw in charcoal if I was in a life-drawing class. One line stretches down from between my legs towards my feet and separates as it reaches my lower calves, and the second is from where one of my breasts is pressing down onto the other, creating a dolphin-type smile. One line points towards my feet and the other up towards my nose. Fainter lines are scored over my hips as if markings left by an unknown tribe.

I am beautifully simple, it seems, and this moment would remain lovely and calm if I didn't see that again my stomach is odd, bulging more than usual and unnaturally so.

Our room appears aged, with the light of day being squeezed out, the outside pushing in. The chest of drawers is flat in this light, two-dimensional as if it was painted scenery for a pantomime. The room is not as alive as me and yet I realise that we are one and the same. The particles which make up the sheet down around my knees and the air are dancing in and out of each other's space, causing the line which separates the sheet from the air to appear blurry. And the shapes which are my legs have fragmented and are dotting about, mingling with the wardrobe door. I pull the sheet back up to contain myself and it rests on me and I don't know why I am surprised that the sheet should stay there like it's been told to sit and stay. Why should the sheet adhere to the laws of gravity? For all I know the sheet might be a dog as much as it might be a sheet and I could be an odd-shaped mattress, stuffed with springs.

How confusing it is that I am watching my own face. Double vision. I should wear a patch like the singer who has that wandering eye. I am all inside out and my seams are seamless. It's easier when things are outside in, I mean the right way round.

And how quiet it all is. The Sea View Hotel is still, no footsteps on the stairs or slamming of doors or laughter from one drink too many too early or bickering about where the key is in the room and you had it last. The rest of the Sea View Hotel might not exist if I open the door. There could just be a long drop down to a bombed-out hole and me standing in a doorway in the wind looking out and yet looking back at myself.

People say they wake up on the ceiling peering down at the person they know as themselves and panic that they might have died. But, with my pink cheeks, I am clearly alive, doubly alive, me and me, maybe that's what they mean when someone says I feel more alive than ever.

My mouth is slightly open and I am breathing gently in and out. I get up close and see I have soft blonde fur along the top of my lip which I bet gets illuminated in the sunshine. No one has ever told me if it does that and I bet even if they've seen it they wouldn't say it to me, as people are taught to be good and not say things that could be counted as rude.

Women are taught it is wrong to have hair in the places which men are allowed it, like chins, underarms, legs and upper lips. I wouldn't mind knowing what it felt like to stroke my own beard. Hairy nipples are a definite no-no and must be plucked out immediately, it says in one of Petula's magazines. Even men are starting to wax their chests and their balls. It seems the lot of us are purposefully becoming hairless, apart from on our heads, where it is against the law for a woman to not have hair or a wig. My hair is really thick. Hairdressers have said so, they go, isn't your hair lovely and thick, while thinning it with their scissors.

I'm out of sorts. My abdomen is bulging and my breasts are sore. I can feel it all and I can see it all under the sheet. I exist while watching myself exist, a double gaze, a mirror, my eyes confirm the real ones.

And suddenly, as the light becomes a little darker in the room as if on a dimmer switch, I am uncomfortable with all of this and I know it isn't normal and want to go back inside my body in case I am dead and there hasn't yet been enough time to turn blue.

23

The curtains are not pulled and the light from the street is lying across my feet. It is a sort of warped rectangular orange shape with the folds of the net curtain in it. I'm awake, with one hand over half of my face, over one eye, like a person with a migraine in a black room. I remove my hand and blink until I am properly awake. I see it is properly dark outside, so that means I have been in bed all day sleeping, that is if it *is* still today.

I feel sick and I remember it must be to do with my swollen stomach. It's making me feel really weird. I've got the sense that I could be pregnant, that this could be what it's like. But that would be stupid, I mean incredible, wouldn't it? Maybe I've just got really bloated from all the vodka I drank and I've got one of those twisted guts from all the stress, or maybe it's wind.

But don't women say they just know? They wake up and know and don't need a doctor or wee on a pregnancy stick to know it's true. The younger ones who drink coffee in the caff told me that knowing you are pregnant is like meeting the one, you'll just know when it happens, they say, you know and it's so simple and clear that your own feelings are the writing on the pad, the proof, the hard evidence, as those sorts of feelings never lie. But on the other hand you get the women who say that they didn't know they were expecting and don't feel a thing until one day they are sat on the toilet and a baby comes out and the headline in the newspaper is 'I GAVE BIRTH TO A BABY BOY AND DIDN'T EVEN KNOW I WAS PREGNANT!' The babies must be as small as tadpoles, their mothers' wombs squashed by silence, or maybe they just aren't very in touch with their feelings, which is difficult to imagine since we are of the age when all feelings are dissected like frogs at school.

Maybe it's like most things that seem hard to believe at the time, like you leaving us and Simon being a woman and Sally not giving two hoots about me, they become less strange after a while, when you've settled into the idea of them. Me being pregnant might be just like that, bizarre one day, normal the next. Just like when something is complete, but you don't know it is until it's broken and then soon after you get so used to the broken thing you can't recall it otherwise.

Oh God. I think I am pregnant.

Now, if you were here and you could speak you might ask me, why do you think you are pregnant, and I would say, because, and not in a defensive moody teenager sort of way, but simply because I do. Because there is a full feeling there which is not from eating too much; it's like my body has made its mind up, if a body can have a mind of its own. And if I think about it, it was there yesterday but not fully formed, and so it is only right that it has taken shape now, today, as if it's been a while coming. Something is fitting about its timing. Something has been building up, layer on layer, and it is separate from me but at the same time identical to me. And apart from this sensation, which can only be described inadequately as the something or the lump below or the feeling, there are physical signs to consider. Like I've skipped my period twice and I want garlic bread in the middle of the night and I can see my breasts are dangling, blown up and enlarged with nipples as big as the tops of my fingers, and I have had all those mornings when I felt nauseous serving up fried, scrambled or poached breakfasts.

And those cravings, they are nothing new. I've had a long relationship with them. Fill yourself up with your favourite thing until you can't stand it any longer is one of my great pastimes, like when I used to watch the first bit of *The Sound of Music* eating apples and sucking cough sweets. Holding the cough sweet on one side of my mouth while I chewed the apple on the other with the volume turned up created an incredible confusion of the senses. But I suppose cravings are cravings because you aren't allowed to have the thing which you crave all the time (Mum didn't let me have cough sweets too often). Cravings are linked with desire and there's nothing that you want more when you can't have it, possess it. Sally became a craving straight away. It's a shame she isn't available in a packet in the corner shop.

I start to imagine cold cucumbers and chocolate eclairs sliced up into large mouth-size chunks so the cream will get all over my face. Cheesecake without berries on top with squirty cream and chicken korma with a bubbled nan bread, Chinese food which comes in boxes that they pick at in American comedies, Yorkshire pudding and gravy, watermelon slices or roasted potatoes covered in salt and crisp apple strudel.

I suppose from now on doctors will tell me to put my feet up as much as I like, and people will give up their seat for me on the bus. And very soon I might have small printed pictures from those ultrasound scans, like the mothers do who sit in the caff cooing, which I will put in a book and when I am old I will look over them and be amazed at how the baby was once the size of a two-penny piece. And unlike Mum I would never throw anything away. I would cast my baby's first shoes in bronze and have a lock of its baby hair so I could sniff that baby smell over and over.

I suppose I should try and think about how this happened. I mean, how this could really be true since I haven't had sex with a man. Now something could have happened when I was drunk, or maybe I was abducted in my sleep by a sperm-shooting alien. And what if that stranger who I woke up with in my flat had been a he? I mean, I was never sure what had happened and I only assumed she didn't have a penis. She could have done something to me before we passed out. And then there was that time which I wasn't going to mention when I went back for a drink with the woman who lived above the kebab shop who had no furniture and

I realised hadn't washed for a long time when I got closer to her and smelt her and it made me feel sick, but I let her touch me anyway as I wanted to be touched. What if she'd slipped something up?

But as much as I search for a moment of possible conception I know deep down that it all began with Sally and it'll probably end without her and if anything at all, all of this is because of her. Everything is about her. So as much as I don't want to think or talk about her any more, I will have to go over the story one more time. The beginning.

It is a good one though, I think you'll agree.

24

It started with a sandwich.

Ruby was out at a hospital appointment to do with a lump which thankfully came to nothing. Elsie was waiting tables trying to help out and had so far only dropped one dirty plate, making all the customers jump and stop eating, knives and forks in hand, until she had brushed it up. We were coping, but I was a bit behind with the orders. I remember the time as the two o'clock news had just come onto the radio and the elections had started in the US and there was another demonstration in New York about the war in Iraq. I was cutting up three squares of lasagne from the big tray and had one eye on the chips. They were interviewing a woman who said she wanted America to wake up and see what their president was doing. She sounded young and excited and very far away. I imagined the streets of New York like on the beginning of *Cagney and Lacey* when the pretty blonde one is jogging and she stops to buy a hot dog and I was thinking about how the hot dogs in New York must taste really good.

And then I looked up and the girl who I came to know as Sally was in front of the counter with a scarf up around her ears and taking off her gloves. Her nose was pink from the cold and her blue eyes were watering. They were as blue as the shallow end of the new local pool. She ordered while removing her scarf, revealing shoulder-length golden-blonde hair with the glossy texture found only on hair-dye boxes. I asked her to sit down and wait and I would call her. I asked her her name and wrote it down on the pad which has two bits to every order and the one on the bottom is a duplicate.

'Sally,' she'd said with a lisp. The 's' was pronounced in the voice of a snake.

1 x cheese and onion roll to t/away.

I made her wait until I had finished all the other orders before I started buttering her roll, hoping that she might decide to take her coat off. She didn't, she just sat and read a book. It was a poetry book and I could tell because there was a lot of blank space on the pages. While I was serving up, I kept one eye on her to see if she was looking at me and I could feel that when I had my head down she was and when I lifted up my head she put hers down. It was the best game I had ever played. Only once did I catch her eye and it made my stomach flip. But then I realised she could have been looking at me because she was wondering where her cheese roll was.

When I had finished the roll and wrapped a serviette round it and put it in a white paper bag and swung it over itself, holding the corners like greengrocers do with tomatoes, I called her name.

Sally.

She looked up and pushed back her chair and I wish the moment could have gone in slow motion as it would have done in a romantic film, as it was all over too fast. Before I knew it, her money was in my hand and she was walking out of the door, my eyes following her slim hips and the pockets on the back of her jeans. I kicked myself for missing the opportunity as I could have written my number on the paper bag or something funny like 'eat me'.

Ruby returned looking worried as she wouldn't get her results for a week, and I had my break. I sat down with Simon's journal, looking for clues as to where he might be hiding. I had cheese on toast and was being careful not to let the butter drip onto his writing. He had always written in tiny handwriting, packing the sentences so tightly together so as to not leave any room, nowhere to read between the lines. Most of it was too small to decipher and there seemed to be a lot of codes and abbreviations so whoever found it (probably Mum) wouldn't be able to unlock it. What I could read was written the previous year and was mostly about Amanda and how she wanted to do things like go shopping in a woollen skirt or to the cinema with a boy and snog in the back row and if only she had longer eyelashes. If you didn't know, you would think Amanda was his best friend as it is written in the third person. He says one day Amanda would like to go skiing in salopettes and she thinks most women don't care enough about how they look. And yet even though I was concentrating on Simon, my mind kept flitting back to the moment Sally had walked in and had sat down, actually here in Ruby's caff, her entrance creating a shimmering effect like heat distorting the air above the tarmac in summer. I looked at the chair which she had sat on and how it hadn't been properly pushed back in yet and I decided I would leave it like that for as long as possible. That moment was as miraculous as a magician's trick, one minute she was there, the next she'd gone.

I closed my eyes and made a wish. I put all my thoughts into the words and repeated them, wishing she would come back in for another roll, or even better a cup of tea which she would sit and drink, leaving her lipstick on the edge for me to look at when she had gone. Sally come back, Sally come back, Sally come back.

And sure enough, as they say, as corny as in a predictable movie, she did come back – later that day with a bag full of groceries – and she ordered a cup of tea which I served to her. She'd taken off her grey woollen coat. Underneath was a blue V-necked jumper which dipped down low enough to get a glimpse of her hilly breasts.

'I've left the tea bag in,' I said, not knowing what to say. 'We do that here, so people have the choice.' My words were running away from me.

She'd smiled up at me and her eyes crinkled at the sides.

'That's good. To have a choice, I mean,' she said.

I thought that was very deep, what she'd said, as those words made me think that the world was a place with never-ending opportunities as if I was an astronaut looking down from the moon and I wasn't too old to become a ballet dancer if I still wanted to.

She drank her tea and I was trying not to watch, even though when I stood with my back to her at the counter I could still see her. Her hands were remarkable. Squarer than you'd imagine, with long, strong fingers. The sort which could dig and rustle in the earth for potatoes. When she looked like she had finished I plucked up the courage to go over and take the mug.

'Thank you,' she said. 'Have you worked here long?'

I realised she was attempting a conversation with me which made me feel excitedly awkward and hold my stomach in.

'Quite a while,' I said, thinking about it. 'About a year.'

Silence. Oh no, what should I say, something please something come to mind.

'Do you go out round here?' she said.

'No. It's not got any good bars really, just old men's pubs,' I said.

'Do you fancy going out for a drink?' she said as bold as anything.

'Well. Yes, I think I'd like that,' I said, feeling a bit faint.

'I'll wait for you to finish up if you like,' she said, looking up momentarily and putting a spoon in the mug and stabbing at the used bag.

'OK, I'll ask Ruby if I can get away a bit early.' I turned round and raced over to the counter and banged into a chair with my hip, which really hurt but I didn't let on. The chair made a farting noise on the laminated flooring as I did so and I blushed, hoping she hadn't thought it was me. Ruby smiled at me when I asked if I could leave ten minutes early and looked over my shoulder and then said yes, since I had covered for her when she had her appointment. She told me to take care as I left, in a way now I realise was a caution, and Sally and I got on a bus to a bar in between where she and I live called the Pink Panther.

So, in the Pink Panther I tried to impress Sally and she just let me talk. My ears were very hot for the first hour or so until I forgot about them. Sally said I needed a scarf for winter. She asked a question every time I had finished my sentence and I was thinking how well the conversation was going even though I wasn't learning anything about her. She was older than me. Close up, her laughter lines were apparent when she didn't laugh and she was confident and self-assured in the way she didn't feel she had to speak when I couldn't think of what to say next. I told her about Simon, but tried to make out I wasn't that upset about it. I told her about Petula and how she was addicted to sex, as I thought it would make her laugh. She asked me if I had been involved with anyone before and I said nothing serious in a way which would make her think I had. We had five rounds of drinks, taking it in turns to go to the bar. She bought the first and the last and the one in the middle which meant I owed her one, but I was relieved that she said we should go after five as I only had enough money left for my bus fare home.

I also told Sally about my love of photography. I had tried to make myself more interesting than I was by telling her about the different types of cameras I'd collected and how I was refusing to go digital as I liked the smell of film and the way you can touch it. I told her how digital wasn't solid enough for me as I would all too easily erase everything and then what would be left? Plus I don't have a computer as that would be a luxury and the Internet would take over my life. She laughed and said I didn't need a computer as I could get all my photos put onto disks at a photo place but she didn't seem to understand the satisfaction I got from being able to handle film and the negatives. She didn't get the way I liked to hold the negatives up to the light to find the right one and how interesting it is to see a negative where everything's dark where it really is light. Where it's all back to front and how it isn't about something being necessarily easy or modern. She seemed into the subject enough though, and said how she thought it was good to have a passion and that she would like me to take her photo. I imagined her posing nude on a chaise longue and eating grapes with a sheet draped over, suggesting no knickers. I had asked her what her passion was and she hadn't replied. Instead, she'd leant back and looked me in the eye, directly without fear, up and down.

After we had finished our drinks and put on our coats I had said thank you for a lovely evening and she had said well, do you want it to be over? I squirmed and said no, not really and she took my hand and we left the Pink Panther and at last I was a sensational hit and I enjoyed the exiting of a pub for the first time, wishing I could show off Sally's hand in mine to the people sat on the high stools at the bar. I felt a little famous.

At the bus stop she kissed me, pressing me onto the sliding red seat with the plastic glass and the bus routes behind my back. When I opened my eyes I saw that a man was watching us, but then I closed them again as she pressed her soft open lips against mine, lifting my chin so I got neck ache. A while later, when I reopened my eyes he had gone and she wet her thumb and took my face in her hands and said, 'Hold on a minute,' and she dabbed under my eye and said, 'Look, it's one of yours.' And there was one of my eyelashes stuck to her thumb and she pulled open her pocket and let it drop in there. I wanted to follow.

We got the bus to Sally's house which meant we were going further away from mine. When we got in she opened a bottle of wine and we sat on her sofa and she balanced her wine glass on my knee. I wanted to ask her questions but she didn't seem to want to talk any more. She just pushed me back on the sofa and lay on top of me. I was amazed at how grown-up her house was – she even had a proper mantelpiece – and surprised that, although she was shorter and thinner than me, she felt heavier as if her body was packed tighter together.

The next morning I barely knew who I was.

The arrival of two Hawaiian pizzas at the door (with that exotic pineapple) was the only reason Sally got up that day. I hadn't been back to my flat and I had got out of bed only to use the toilet and have a quick shower. She had a lovely white duvet set with matching pillowcases and I had nearly lost my appetite for the first time in my life. I was careful not to get pizza on the duvet cover and instead had dropped it on my chest and she licked it off.

The morning after the Pink Panther, I had phoned in sick to the caff. Ruby could tell from my voice that I wasn't ill, but I felt like nothing mattered except Sally. I hadn't even bothered to put on the sore-throat voice that I've used before in other jobs. This was like a dream, but I was awake and I knew I had to make the most of it as it might disappear at any moment. I didn't want to waste any of it.

We drank black coffee as there was no milk left and I didn't want to leave the house for the shop.

She had lifted my arms above my head and pressed my hands into the pillows, looking down at me, and kissed me all over, over and over again. And it's as if this was how she communicated, through sex. She wanted more and more and interrupted my conversations with her trowel-like hands. When the motorbike pulled up outside and the doorbell bing-bonged, I watched her getting out of the bed to get the pizzas, wrapping her Chinese dressing gown over her body and when she'd left the room, I'd lain there knowing that the bolt-of-lightning-out-of-the-sky saying was true. Here she was, all I had been looking for without knowing it, the person that made me complete and full, full to bursting. So there you go, I guess that was when it happened, the conception, right then, when I found a place where I belonged, where I felt right, a tiny piece of home.

The address was Sally.

When I said goodbye the next morning I felt as if we were leaving each other forever; it tore me apart. I was willing to phone in sick once more but Sally, quite abruptly, had said no and that she had to go to work. She said I had to too.

It was a Monday and sleet was melting on people's spiky black umbrellas.

From leaving her at her front door, I wanted the time to disappear between saying goodbye and saying hello. Down the road, a little away from that first goodbye, two minutes from kissing it on her lips, I had sent her a text message saying 'Missing you already XXX'.

Four minutes passed before she responded and then she texted back 'me too' but with a small x. During those four minutes, under the shadow of the Crystal Palace tower, after me pressing Send and her replying, I kept my phone in my hand, checking it every few seconds to see if that small envelope had appeared in the corner of the screen and 1 Message Received would show in the middle in a box of its own. In those two-hundred and forty seconds I had thought that maybe she didn't really like me or she'd thought something awful about me as I left and changed her mind and I felt embarrassed that my words had been so carefree and that I should have waited at least another ten minutes, so I didn't seem so keen. But then when she did reply the beep made me jump and I saved it in a file which I named Sally. But even then I worried about the size of her kiss and how it never got any bigger than a small x and mine just got more and more and always in capitals.

I wanted rid of that time between the goodbye and the hello (but then felt bad about all the terminally ill people who just pray for more time). I felt as if I was the only one in the world feeling this, who had ever felt like this, and I wanted to shake the people in the street and ask them if they were feeling anything at all. They all looked bored and preoccupied with whether the bus was coming. I'm sure my heart was visible, right on the end of my sleeve.

Ruby was cross, when I first arrived at work. She handed me my freshly pressed apron and made me clean the grill. She asked me with a darted look if I was feeling any better and was I expecting to be ill again soon as she'd had to ring for help from Julie, who used to work here before she went funny. I said no and felt bad and realised that love would have to be kept for the evenings and my one day off a week.

Work dragged and the clock stopped ticking when I stared at it, willing it to speed up. I put the radio on Heart FM and every song meant something to me. I had to wait a whole other meaningless eight hours before I could see her again.

I asked Ruby if my one day off could become a Sunday and she said yes, provided that I was honest with her in the future, which made me feel bad all over again. She put a sign with Part-time Waitress Required Within written in black marker pen.

I knew I was forgiven later that day when she gave me two portions of apple pie to take home.

25

The taste of treacle tart is in my mouth and I know I have to get out of this bed and this hotel room and have a drink and something to eat before I sink.

I think I've been hallucinating or telling myself a bad joke.

I get up and flip on the main light switch by the door and the objects in the room become solid once more. The firm outline of the chest of drawers is correct and I see Petula's make-up bag and do up the zip. I unplug her hair-straighteners and wrap the cord around the handles and put them back into her wheelie bag. I drop the vodka bottle we hardly touched into her bag and then pull off my clothes from the night before. They still smell of smoke. I have a clean pair of jeans with me in my bag and a T-shirt which smells of washing powder. I take a towel from the toilet-wardrobe and wrap it round my body, holding the little rectangular bar of soap from the sink as I creep out into the corridor. I find the hallway light switch which you push in and which later pops out, as it is on a timer. Room number 11 is silent and I go into the shower room next to it, waving my hand in the dark to find the cord to turn the light on. An extractor fan starts up and the light bulb is really bright, showing all the cracks in the ceiling. There is chequered lino on the floor, curling up around the edge of the shower unit, and mildew spots at the bottom of the shower curtain. I turn the knob of the shower and wait for the right temperature. It is warm enough but a pathetic amount of water drops out. Just enough to get me wet arm by arm, leg by leg. I soap my enlarged belly, watching the suds form as I rub it in circular motions. The water plops down over the bump onto my legs, taking the soap to my feet. It is still there. So here it is. I am a plastic container with a tight-shutting lid holding what Sally did to me for as long as it takes. I wonder if it will be the conventional nine months, as this isn't really that conventional at all.

My mind is now racing and I am worried that I'm going to be responsible for the next Virgin birth. No one would believe me if I told them what I truthfully thought had happened, would they, even if I could? That Sally has caused this in me, caused me to fertilise myself like one of those fish who live in the dark at the bottom of the ocean. The scientists with their proof or the Christians with their big book would all shout that it was impossible. They would say look at who she is, she works in a caff and has only had one day trip to France in her whole life, let alone a holiday in Israel which is where the last one was born. She is hardly suitable to bear the next coming.

In this day and age, once it is born I would be famous and have to appear in *Hello!* magazine and let people see my flat and how I haven't bothered putting up curtains. Mind you, I can't really see the magazine wanting my story. I mean, I am a woman who is in love with a woman (who is now not in love with me), giving birth to an unfertilised thing, which I think started to grow when she saw the woman she loved eat lasagne erotically with a man.

I decide that to bring up this little mystery without being swamped by journalists I will have to escape to a place where people live in teepees and ask no questions, maybe Cornwall, and that stops me racing ahead for a while.

The shower continues to drip after I turn it off and I am careful not to let the mouldy curtain touch my leg as I get out. With the towel wrapped tightly around me I run from the shower room back into the bedroom and shut the door. After the warm shower I notice it's freezing in here again and I shiver and hurry to get my clothes on. Pulling my woollen socks on makes me feel a little more stable.

The act of getting dressed somehow pushes me back into myself as if the process of putting on my clothes tucks me in. The bedroom light helps me see where my edges are and where the rest of the room begins. My hands pull down my jumper and rest on the swelling for a while.

I go over to the bedside table and check my mobile for a message from Petula. There isn't one. She can get the key from reception if she comes back and I borrow one of her jumpers and stuff it under the one I'm wearing to keep the something warm. It feels good there. I tie up my mac loosely and leave the room. Down the steep uneven staircase I imagine I am waddling a little, walking as if I need more room between my legs. I have left the zip and button undone on my jeans as they are uncomfortable done up. I hold on tightly to the staircase rail as it would be all so easy to let it go wrong at this early stage if I should fall. The steps are wonky and my feet tread carefully until I reach the bottom step where I can smell the hot odour of boiled sheets. The woman at reception only vaguely lifts her head as I put the room key on the counter.

Already it is dark and the world rushes past getting ready for the Saturday night ahead. I have that feeling as if I have just left a cinema and it was light when I went in and now it's dark. The night is surprising and it's as if time has escaped me. A whole week could have passed, but I know it hasn't as the landlady would have been at the door and Petula would have been back for her make-up bag and hair tongs.

The restaurant I sit in has no name, just a colour scheme. Earthy browns and kidney reds echo the interior of my proud new insides. I am sat on a square leather pouffe. The waiter moved a chair aside for me when he showed me to my table, as if he was taking special care of me. He has sat me in the No Smoking section near a family with a pushchair, away from a group of people who seem a bit drunk and from the way they are reclining on the leather sofas, have been there all afternoon. Before I sit down I look in the pushchair and ask how old the baby is. I've never done this in my life. I have never been interested before and it feels as if I am speaking from a script. The mother smiles and says he is three months and I grin back at her, feeling as if I could be a member of the Family Club which is more important than the Drinking All Afternoon Club. I want to ask her what it's like, if she got piles from all the straining and would she recommend drugs for the birth or one of those natural ones in a paddling pool; but their food comes.

The menu arrives with the waiter and I order onion rings for starters and garlic bread. Then I have a lasagne with a green leafy side salad and apple pie and custard for dessert and a decaf latte with cream squirted on top to finish.

Throughout my meal I watch the parents next to me and worry how worn out they look. They don't seem to talk to one another but communicate through passing various items to each other for the baby. The mother hands a tissue to the father to wipe the snot running from the baby's nose, who then wipes it and puts it in his pocket. When the baby wakes up, the father passes the baby to the mother and she passes him back the baby's coat. On the table they have an immaculate Saturday newspaper still in its plastic cover, a ritual of theirs now postponed for the immediate future.

By the time I am ready to leave the restaurant the family has left as the baby started to wail, but before they went, they glanced down at my stuffed jumper and wished me luck. I liked them and wished I knew where they lived. We could have been friends and I might have picked up some tips. As I push open the door to the restaurant I realise I am facing the direction of the sea. People are rushing by and one man knocks into me, slightly spinning me off my feet, and he doesn't say sorry. The cars seem inexplicably loud as if the volume in the street has been turned up. I put my hands over my ears and my hands become like conch shells and I think I can hear the sea twofold.

A woman in a headscarf with a shopping trolley appears and I ask for the directions for back home as I suddenly can't recall where I am. She says she doesn't know where my home is and she stares at my face and asks me if I am all right, but it sounds like she is asking the question from a very faraway place and I am sinking without being in water and before I know it I am on the floor and I have gone.

26

I haven't been in hospital since I tried to eat a china cup. It was fine porcelain with a gold trim and flowers on the outside and so fragile and precarious that it made me want to bite into it. It reminds me now of the feeling I get when I see babies' feet.

The hospital stay was enjoyable, as Simon brought me a picture he'd drawn of me and him leaving the hospital in a car, me with a big bandage on my face and him with long green shoes which reached the bottom of the paper. The proportions were all wrong, making the bandage and the shoes the most obvious things in the picture. I'd stayed in overnight; the ward was too big for our small beds and they kept the lights on all night, just in case. The next morning Simon and Mum were the first to arrive and came especially early, and I had that being famous feeling when they walked in, past the other children who looked on with no one sitting in their visitors' chairs. Mum stroked the hair from off my face, peering down at me, brought Lucozade in rustly orange cellophane and I bet she only did that because she felt she was being watched by the nurses. When they left, the table that goes across the bed had the Get Well card on it from Simon and a smaller one with a kitten on it from Mum. Although I wasn't ill, they pretended I was as it was easier than asking why I bit the cup in the first place. Mum called it an accident, but I don't think it was.

There were other children there with their legs in plaster with writing and drawings on which made me want to break something of mine, and some who looked perfectly all right and like they were just sitting in hospital beds for no reason at all. One girl cried all the time and the nurse stayed with her and she had to eat cotton-wool sandwiches as she had swallowed a lollipop stick. Not an ice-lolly stick like the doctor uses to hold down your tongue to examine your throat, but a white thin one which was satisfying to unpeel when wet.

Mothers say 'accidents will happen, you know' as if it's a prediction, a certainty, but then they only say it after an accident has happened.

The nurse explained that they wanted the cotton wool to go down into her stomach and wrap itself around the stick so it wouldn't poke holes in her stomach. Luckily I didn't swallow the piece of china, which stayed in my mouth as Mum tried to stop the blood from dripping on the carpet with a tea towel. Now I can put my finger in my mouth and trace the scar on the inside of my cheek. That's how I know that it really happened. And you know, I hadn't expected it to hurt.

Today I am in a hospital ward with six beds; each set of two is facing each other and plugged into my wrist hidden by a plaster is a tube which is attached to a drip. The drip is a pouch of clear-looking liquid hanging from a stand. Depending on what I do with my hand I can speed up or slow down the rate of the drip. Next to the stand is a locker with a jug with a blue lid on it full of water from the hospital taps. Everyone gets the same. There is a small plastic beaker next to it and I bet it's that size so that no one can take big gulps and make themselves sick. The door of the locker is open and inside I can see a clear plastic bag with my clothes in it and I am relieved to see something familiar, something that is mine. Almost touching the locker is a closed curtain around the bed next to me and I can hear a man behind it talking in hushed tones. He is having a one-sided conversation. Later, when the curtain is swished back by the nurse I will see that in the bed is an old woman, his wife, who looks fed up and tells me she wants to be left alone. It is really hot in here and I pull back the sheet to cool down. The something is still there underneath a white gown which ties up at the back. My leg is bruised and my hand is grazed. I have no shoes or socks on but my knickers are still there where they should be.

The nurse walks in. Her dress is comfortingly tight across her body. She is checking the notes at the ends of the beds of the women opposite me. I can see graphs. The old women are all asleep and so old-looking they might as well be dead. When she arrives at the end of my bed she picks up the clipboard which hangs on the bottom bar and says, 'Now in the land of the living, I see. How are you feeling?'

'I'm not sure really,' I reply. My voice sounds strange, as if it's coming out of a speaker near my head. She is black and has a gentle accent I suspect is from seas much more turquoise than the Brighton one, although a Caribbean patch does appear to the left of the pier on a good day, even in winter. I like the way her body fits into the nurse's dress, all compact as if her body is made for the dress rather than the other way round. Later she tells me she is from Barbados and her favourite food is sweet potato roasted with nutmeg.

'Now, honey, we need some information from you, if you are feeling up to it.'

She comes and perches on the bed by my feet.

'We know your name from what was on your bank card. But we haven't got your home address. You don't seem to be registered from round here. Are you on your holidays?'

My home. Where is it? It comes back to me.

'The Sea View Hotel,' I say.

'Uh-huh,' she says, eyeing me cautiously. 'And is that where you are on holiday?'

'No . . . I live above Petula.'

My mind was finding it difficult to remember the address or my date of birth. What was the colour of my front door? Did I have a front door?

'And is Petula your friend?'

'Yes,' I say. I think so.

'Can we call Petula, or is there anyone else who should know where you are?'

Anyone else, I thought, anyone else, and then it came to me, her face.

'You could call Sally Hunter. She's my friend and she's at the Royal Albion Hotel with a man. Petula is at the Sea View with me, by the sea, you know near the front.'

'OK.' She pauses, studying her notes. 'I'll see if I can contact either of them. Once you've seen the doctor tomorrow for your blood results you should be free to go home, but you will need someone to help you, as you are very weak.'

'What day is it?' I say, as I need to be placed somewhere firmly.

'Sunday. It's a Sunday.'

I know it's not right to mention Sally and I don't know why I did. I suppose I think if she finds out I am in hospital she will be concerned and come and visit with a card and a bunch of flowers, scared I could be dying. Then she'll know I'm pregnant and we can raise it together in a house which smells of baking and towels drying on the radiator.

And then the nurse says, 'Have you had a pregnancy test?' her eyes softening and looking down at my body, trying to work me out.

I don't know what to say, so I say nothing and then I ask how come I am here? And she tells me the short story of how I got there. She starts with the ambulance man. According to him, my story begins when I collapsed in the street and a lady phoned an ambulance (who I remember now must have been the lady with the headscarf) and that I was brought to the hospital in Brighton where I wasn't conscious but I was breathing and I came round and said please look after my baby and then went again and they found out from doing some tests that I was severely dehydrated and anaemic.

It's not a great story and fairly disappointing in the end.

Sometime later, they have taken another blood sample and I

have had an examination with the curtain pulled round the bed where a silent doctor snapped surgical gloves on and felt deep inside me and nodded at the student nurses, saying my cervix was swollen, indicating that I was about six weeks pregnant but we would have to wait for the results of the blood test. Then, with his hairy eyebrows knotted and looking in my direction, he said that I must really start to look after myself, in a tone which insinuated that he blamed me for wasting NHS time and money.

So it is true. I am pregnant. The doctor has confirmed it. It should be amazing news and I am relieved that he has validated everything I suspected but, thinking about it, I am pregnant by unnatural means and I'm not sure now whether it is good or bad news. I can't get excited surrounded by the grey ladies in their nighties or the hospital curtain hooks.

How could this have happened? Maybe Sally shot some sperm into me with a turkey baster when I wasn't looking. But that is ridiculous, as she would have asked first and there was very little time that I didn't look. Lying here in the strip-lit ward, it is not as thrilling and weird as it would be if I were starring in a film where everyone knew that I hadn't slept with the leading man or any of the extras. The audience, I expect, would be fascinated by the surreal quality of my pregnancy, though it might have to be an art-house movie playing to a group of film buffs. But there is no audience, and no one is interested in me, apart from the Caribbean nurse who is paid to be interested, so I will pretend that this is all ever so normal, that I am ever so normal. After all I, the pregnant woman, am not unusual in a hospital, where birth and death are as commonplace as the chips I serve at Ruby's caff. But I am sure that if they knew my story, I would be given my own special room with a box television.

There will be no press yet, no flash photography and no news reportage with furry microphones. They will not appear until I am really showing or the test has come back to verify what I already know to be true.

Later a woman comes around with food on a trolley. There are plates with metal lids on to keep the heat and moisture in and underneath my lid is macaroni cheese. It's a bit dry, but then we have pudding and a cup of tea which makes up for it. Visitors come but no one comes for me and the nurses change shifts and no one comes for me. The Caribbean nurse has changed into a Scottish nurse, who replaces my pouch. The visitors who have come mostly leave and I find it difficult to concentrate. My mouth is dry and I hold on to my something as if it's the only thing left apart from the clothes in my cupboard, and I realise if I had the strength I would be worrying now. I would be fretting about where Petula was and if she could be contacted and if she doesn't go back to the hotel tomorrow all our stuff will be thrown away. But I don't have enough energy to really get into my normal way of thinking.

The blood-test results will be back the next day they say, but they don't once comment on the pregnancy and speak only about my kidneys and the dehydration, which surely could be sorted out with a few glasses of water.

I fell over and passed out and I wonder if anyone laughed at me. Falling over must happen all the time. Across the world how many people trip or topple in one single day? I can see it now like a quick-edited film, children running too fast in playgrounds, people slipping over uneven kerbs and dips in the street, women with spiky shoes stuck in the grates of drains, skiing holiday capers and ice-skating slip-ups. Old people with bad hips trying to get out of their chairs must do it every second, but then it's called 'having a fall'.

People laugh when you fall over. I'm not sure if they always have or why it's funny, it just is. It's not good to laugh at the old dears with their bones as brittle as chicken wishbones, but, unlike falling in love, falling over is amusing to others. It's silly, but that TV programme which is made up entirely of people and animals having mishaps unexpectedly caught on camera makes me laugh.

I've giggled at it before with Petula on an early Saturday evening before going out, our dinner trays on our laps. Cats falling off the backs of sofas and babies falling off of swings or just sitting and toppling over on the carpet, energetic wedding guests dancing wildly and bringing down several others when they tumble, and the child who falls off the stage during the school nativity play. Nowadays, people make their accidents happen on purpose for the camera so that they earn money from it.

I don't think watching myself falling over would be funny, now I know what it's like, unless it was shown on TV and I got the money for it. There's a sort of cruelty to that programme when you think about it.

On each knee I have a plaster. I thought grazed knees and plasters were the territory of children. I guess that's why it's such a shocking thing to fall over and get grazed knees again when you're all grown up. It makes you realise how little you can be at any time in your life.

27

The hospital keeps the lights on in the ward all night. Illness never stops and only by the absence of visitors do I guess it's the middle of the night.

I can't ever recall sleeping properly, all those nights I spent with Sally. I would look at her eyelids shimmering with her thin application of night-time eye gel and think how lucky I was. Occasionally she would open her eyes to see if I was looking at her. I loved watching her sleep, wondering where she went to, but sometimes felt jealous because I couldn't go there with her. Occasionally, I would nudge her with my elbow to bring her back to me. Soon this started to make her turn over and I realised that it was too much to expect her to be awake all the time. If I loved her, I should be considerate and leave her alone to sleep.

So instead I would study the ceiling and the cornice at the top and how the pattern looked like lots of tiny church doorways, and then my eye would wander directly down to the enlarged print of a sunset from a holiday she went on to Africa with the girl who had left bruises on her arms, whom she never mentioned but I knew she was occasionally thinking about. If I had my way, there would be no sunset picture for me to stare at in the middle of the night; I would prefer it to be just wall.

I can recall always waking up just before her, so I must have had a little doze, and looking at her as she woke and feeling that what we had was the rightest thing in the world. So I suppose that's why I shouldn't be surprised that I am pregnant: our love was just as explosive as anyone else's, just as potent. Enough to make the world go round twice as fast in fact.

I get out of bed and take hold of the drip stand and wheel it out into the corridor. The nurses are gathered around a desk chatting and let me walk forward without concerning themselves. My knees are weak and my whole body is dragging down. I think it would rather be on the floor. I find the toilet which has a lot of space in it for wheelchairs and padded handles to hold onto, as if there was a danger of falling off like on a fairground ride. There is a red cord by the toilet in case of emergencies and I am tempted to pull it to see who'll come, but know it would only be a nurse and not Sally who is the one who I really want to save me, as she is the only one that can. I know the person who hurts you is the only one that can take it away.

Perhaps she'll come tomorrow. Maybe she is already planning what she will say: how sorry she is and how she wants me back. No, she won't be coming, will she? I know she'll be in bed with him, letting him watch her as she pretends to sleep.

Sitting on the toilet seat staring ahead at the green handwash dispenser over the sink, I can't be bothered to get up and I want to just sit there and do nothing. I want to stop how I am thinking as I know it's no good. I want to change the record. I know how boring it is and how bored I am of the record. No amount of wishing or wanting will bring her back now. Or you for that matter.

28

I am on my way home on the fast train to Victoria, stopping only at three stops on the way, Gatwick Airport, East Croydon and Clapham Junction. It is one of those new trains with the material on the seats still bristly and no graffiti on the windows. Petula rushed ahead and got us a set of four seats with a table and saved the seats with our bags until I got there. The table in front of me reminds me of the table in the hospital that pulled across me.

It seems that hospital is the worst place to go to feel better as I feel exhausted just from trying to get some sleep, even though I must have slept quite a lot as whole hours have gone missing, but it's not enough. The woman next to me shouted out nurse a lot in the night, even when she didn't really need one. The nurse would come and the woman would say she didn't know what it was she wanted or remember why she'd called her. The other women took it in turns to snore and fidget and sigh and groan.

But today Petula came and found me and is now taking me home.

She was pale and sweaty as she wheeled all our stuff into my view and asked me how I was. She looked tired and concerned and wasn't wearing any mascara so her eyes appeared small. She told me the story of how she'd gone back to the Sea View Hotel on that Sunday morning in time to check out, thinking I would be there waiting for her, and when she realised I wasn't there she thought I'd killed myself and how then she'd got this crazy notion that it was all her fault because she hadn't come back for two nights as she was having such a good time and maybe met The One. Then she'd gone to the police, who'd said the best thing to do was to wait and see if she contacts you in the next twenty-four hours and only then could they fill in a missing person report. And how she'd gone and stood on the pier and looked at the sea, imagining my body being washed up. She told the bouncer how Simon was missing and now it was my turn and what a family we were all to be missing. She told me how much she'd cried and how he'd been really kind to her, holding her hand and staying with her as they'd sat on the white painted benches hoping I'd walk past. And that there was hard house music playing by the fairground rides on the pier which reminded her of when we used to go out clubbing, and she described how the songs had made her feel so bad as we never did that any more and our youth was waning. And how the landlady of the hotel had been no help and couldn't say when she saw me last and just said that Petula had to take all our stuff with her unless she wanted to pay for another night's stay and how Petula had called her a bitch and the bouncer had to step in and explain she was very upset. She held my hand and told me that she wouldn't know what to do if I had died as I was her best friend and she had no one else. And then they had called the hospitals and only that morning had found me.

I didn't tell her my news. That earlier in the morning the blood test had come back negative. I wasn't pregnant; my body had pretended it was. And I didn't tell her that my period had started almost as soon as the doctor had walked off with the information written in his file, and a little later my stomach went down and became soft again. I didn't tell her how I had been crying for ages before she'd got there and the nurse had brought me tea with four sugars and had touched my arm kindly as I sat upright holding the tea, my stomach cramping. How the nurse had said the mind can play tricks on you and that I had what was called pseudocyecis. She wrote it down on a bit of paper for me as not many people would have heard of it and to normal folk it is called a phantom pregnancy, which is not to be confused with a phantom limb which is when an amputee senses his leg or arm is still there, when in physical reality it isn't. But it's all the same sort of thing: the mind creates something which isn't there because it's in a state of confusion, a state of grief.

My body was grieving for my lost love and it had made a baby out of it.

It happened to our dog some years back. The vet had called it a phantom pregnancy, which was ironic since when we tried to look it up in Mum's medical book, which showed actual photographs of people with boils the size of their ears on their faces, it wasn't there. Suzy's little nipples started to swell and she became moody and possessive of her bed. She snarled if we patted her or tried to rub her belly. The vet suggested we make her a litter out of stuffed socks, which we did and she guarded them with a fierce possessiveness. Then one day there was suddenly blood on the sheet Mum had covered the bed with and so the socks were disposed of and she seemed back to her own self again.

The nurse says cattle have been known to have these experiences. Poor cows with their swollen udders and roller-coaster hormones, I'm surprised there isn't more trouble heard of in the countryside. At least I had a nurse to explain it me and bring me a hot drink.

Out of the window of the train the cows stand in the fields rushing past, static like farmyard animals on green felt, and I wonder how they are feeling. If any of them feel like me, all empty and flat and just getting on with the day because it is there.

The train has stopped at the airport and people get on, humping their luggage up the steep step of the train, looking tanned in their T-shirts although it isn't that warm yet. To judge by their clothing, they appear reluctant to leave their holidays behind. Petula for once knows not to speak and sits silently texting next to me. She is leaning into me and I can feel her warmth on my arm. A small girl who probably doesn't go to school yet walks up and stands in the aisle next to us with her mother looking around for a seat and the mother says excuse me which forces Petula to take our bags off the seats so they can sit down. The train is very busy now. The girl is opposite me and is wearing a red coat which her mother unbuttons for her once they are settled. She is staring at me as if she knows something. I look out of the window but keep checking where she is looking by watching her reflection in the window. Her mother gives her a comic and she stops studying me and is looking at the pictures and I recall that Simon and I used to have a comic each to read on the train and how we would swap on the way home so we had each read both. Mum would sit with us and probably unbutton our coats. She must have cared and done all those things a mother does at some point.

The little girl gets off at the next station but one and as she waits for her mother on the platform she turns back to look at me and I poke my tongue out at her, which shocks me more than it does her.

29

'If I am not myself, then the person you are loving is not me.'

This is the last entry in Simon's journal and it is written in red felt-tip pen. I think he meant Mum to find it as he wrote it very clearly in large letters. I have ripped it out and pinned it to my board.

The day after I get home from Brighton I am trying to organise myself. I have put a restraint order on myself from going anywhere near Sally's house. I am not allowing myself out of the local vicinity. If I fail I have to realise that the punishment is in fact how I feel after I've been to Sally's house, utter deflation.

I have my camera out to take to the camera shop and I have the two bits of paper from Brighton, one with the nurse's word on it and the other with Kate the student's number on it. I pin Kate's bit of paper up. I bought the cork pinboard with its cheap pine frame a while back, just after Simon disappeared and just before I met Sally. I wanted to have a place where I could make sense of things, so I could work out where he might be. So I started to collect the things that had been left around me, like the bus ticket with the word bus written on it from the tattooed woman, as if it was a clue. It has been slowly building, like a picture gallery with words and objects, and now there are all sorts of things attached to it and I'm moving them around. Sally's bathroom fluff has been taken from the centre and placed at the edge of the board and I hope she can sense it. Kate's number is now in the centre and underneath is Sally's itinerary with the empty brown film and pubes taped to it and the book of matches from the Royal Albion. Petula's postcard from Wales is up there too.

I like the fact that I have a number on my pinboard to call at my own convenience. That phone number represents another stab at life, it is a number full of hope, it is a brilliant phone number.

I have left the flat and am heading towards the Internet café to look up the nurse's word. Pseudocyecis.

I have never had call to use the Internet before and am feeling a little nervous. I suppose I've been avoiding it. There is a bus from the end of my road which climbs up the hill, past the dinosaurs in the park which only move out of the trees for children and people on the wrong medication, and finishes its journey alongside the Crystal Palace tower at the top. I get off and wander over to the Internet café, which I find out doesn't warrant its name as it doesn't serve food or drinks. It is next to a French café which has French-looking tables and chairs. You can sit outside and look up at the Crystal Palace tower and pretend you are in Paris if you ignore the people. It's across the road from the bus stop, which is still leaning from when a lorry drove into it, the same bus stop that is round the corner from our old house. While I am here, I can check to see if Mum's back at the house and go online all with the same bus fare.

The Internet shop hasn't got an awful lot going on inside. Two men run the place and there are only three computers. I've noticed it is never busy when I've walked past before and I get the feeling it could be a front for something because, as I sit here afraid to ask how to get onto another screen from the first one, two men have come and gone delivering brown envelopes from their jackets without doing any Internetting. Also it is only one pound for an hour so I don't see how they could afford the rent for the place. In the end I ask one of the men to help me. He comes over and leans behind with his two fingers on the mouse, crouching down, making my neck feel tense. He shows me how to double-click the mouse and how I have to click on a blue e to get it all going. Then I can just tap in what I like and things will come up. I thought it would be more like a dictionary with actual pages.

On the Missing Persons website there are all sorts of ordinary-looking people, most of them smiling, each with a small story about where they were last seen and when. Only a few have the red word FOUND printed across their faces. The majority are all still missing but believed to be alive, their families are very hopeful. Curiously, quite a few went missing while in transit. One woman with a brown bob disappeared on a train journey in India and a man dressed in a graduate's gown vanished after not making a flight in New Zealand, but was seen in the airport. Another woman has been missing since 1974 and I can't help but imagine that she must be dead now, or more optimistically, has taken on a very authentic disguise. They have two pictures of her flashing up on the page, one of what she looked like in 1974 and the other a computer image where they have used an age-progression device to show what she would look like now.

I have printed off the form to tell them the details of Simon/Amanda. I am going to send in just the one photo of Amanda and not one of Simon as proof to him that I understand him, should he look on the website. I like the story of the thirty-four-year-old man who was missing for three years and then discovered in a cave in Malta eating plants; his mother went and fetched him home.

It seems from my other research that I had a lucky escape with my phantom pregnancy. Some women's false pregnancies last for a whole nine months or longer, and then there is nothing but thin air to fill up their newly bought Babygros.

I am trying to look at it philosophically; at least I got to know just for a while what it felt like to be pregnant. That is the positive. The negative is that it proves science correct. You do need sperm to make a baby and it can't just happen from loving someone too much.

The Internet says this condition is very rare and there have only been around four hundred cases documented. I wondered who I would call to tell them I should be added to their number. The hospital nurse gave me the number of a grief counsellor to talk to as she said I was likely to feel quite depressed for a while, but I saw one of those once with Simon after you went and it was just a woman who came to our school and we all sat in the nurse's office with a box of man-size tissues on the desk, her wanting us to cry so she felt she had done her job properly.

It was going to take some time to trust my own feelings again. My body took over for a while. It must be how people with cancer feel, as if the body has started doing something completely random of its own accord without asking you what you think, like an unruly child. You would feel betrayed, wouldn't you?

After I'd found out about the women who are so psychologically disturbed that they believe that they've been given secret abortions while under sedation and accuse doctors of taking their foetuses without their knowledge, I leave the Internet place with a new sense of hope from knowing that I have joined the cyber-world and I go to check on Mum's house.

There are two piles of letters on the side now and on top is an Indian menu advertising free delivery with a free bottle of wine for orders over twenty pounds. I study the menu briefly, but as I've lost my appetite I can't get excited over it. It is while I am looking through her uninteresting post that I smell something irregular in the kitchen, like off milk.

I look in the fridge, which is still switched off so no light comes on when I open it, bringing back that uncomfortable wrong feeling. I open the doors to the cupboards, peeping to the back wondering if there could be a dead mouse. There is no gravy mix, no jam and only a few plates left. Then I swing back the lid on the bin to see if there is anything rotting in there. There is nothing but a fresh bin liner, but I do find pieces of what turns out to be two colour photos ripped up into small bits at the bottom of the bin liner and I collect them all up into a white envelope from your old bureau drawer in the dining room and bring them back to my flat. That evening I sit like they do in the movies, under a desk lamp with a pair of tweezers with fresh coffee in the percolator, trying to sort the pieces and fit them all back together. I could have used my fingers but it seemed more scientific that I use tweezers.

At first I think all the fragments are from the same photo, but after a while when I've got all the straight edges put to one side as I used to when starting a jigsaw, I see there were two separate images.

The first is easier to piece together as it is daytime in the photo and there is very little shade. The colours are immediately recognisable as those from outside the front of our house on a sunny day. The eggshell colours of the pebble-dashing, the red-painted brick wall and the long green vase which held umbrellas. Mum is pregnant with Simon in a tan-coloured coat and I am standing beside her holding her hand outside the front gate, the curve over the front door arched just over our heads because you were obviously crouching down to take it. I am looking up at her when I should have been looking ahead at the camera. Mum would have been annoyed at that and we would have had to have a second one taken. It isn't clear what I am thinking but then again photographs won't tell you that. All I can do is look at us and try and work out what is going on. Why we are having our photograph taken at this moment which seems so insignificant when we could just be off to the shops? But then again people take photographs of all sorts of things. Like their anniversary cake amid their anniversary buffet or flowers at a funeral, so at least the flowers stay alive in their memories. We had a man in Ruby's caff the other week who took a photo of his lunch before he ate it.

I have white knee-high socks and shoes with bars that go across the front. My dress looks too small for me or maybe it's because I have my hand up holding Mum's, which has yanked the dress up shorter. She is smiling for you, the sort of smile where she is showing her teeth, and is holding a black handbag which has a thin strap falling from her shoulder. Her coat has big round buttons on the front and it has a tie tied over the lump which is Simon. One of the rips runs down the centre of Mum's face and there is a piece gone astray which I must have dropped or not seen which would have made up one of her eyes. I've looked for it everywhere and have had to give up and admit it must have gone missing like a sock does. Mum's hair looks like it doesn't belong to her. She has big flicks which defy gravity which slide into a bob at the back. At some point later, I found out it was a wig she wore on days when she couldn't be bothered to do her hair. I saw Simon dancing in it through a crack in the door when I was bored of playing in my room. The wig was too big for him and made him appear like he had a shrunken body. He was always a better dancer than me, I noticed, when we went wild to the top forty on a Sunday, I knew I only had one style of dancing and that was all knees and arms.

Mum is pregnant with Simon and looking cheerful and holding my hand. This makes a comfortable padded-booth shape in my mind.

It must have been just before you disappeared and we woke up to Mum crying and banging her head over and over again on the phone receiver in the hallway with a tiny voice at the other end, us not knowing what to do.

The second is of you. And it's now a prize possession regardless of what you're doing in it as it's my only photo of you on your own. Lines where it was ripped form a pattern on it like a splintered windowpane and that's maybe a clue as to how Mum feels, broken up into pieces. Unglued.

The photograph is more difficult to piece together than the other one because it looks like you took it of yourself, on your own without any lights on. There is a lot of black background and your face is a little cut off as you couldn't quite judge where you were pointing the camera at. I've got the upper part of your face complete now and I can't help but study your black pupils and hope that, if I look hard enough, for long enough, I might be able to jump into the image and find out what's going on behind it all, within it. But there is no depth to this photo, I know it is only really a piece of paper.

I've half completed the photo now and I sit back and look at it. The flash has made your face pasty white and your nose is out of focus as it's so close. You are staring straight at the camera with your head tilted up at it as if you are posing for it. It is clearly a private photograph. I can't imagine Mum getting involved with taking it and there wasn't anyone else. The camera could be your secret lover the way you are posing for it. And for some reason as I continue piece by piece I imagine you are not wearing any clothes. You are doing something private for your photograph which I bet you thought would never be seen by anyone else but you and probably wouldn't have been if you hadn't turned into a puff of smoke. Though I don't expect you were expecting to go so soon.

Just before I glue the final piece on which completes your mouth I get the feeling that I shouldn't be looking at the photo at all as, when I've glued it the best I can, I see that your lips are painted red. Parted, pouting and red and there is a little bit of tongue available to see in your mouth.

And I can't stop looking, searching for you in all of this and then I desperately want to find Simon so I can show him.

If only you could speak, now.

30

'You know anal sex is very in at the moment,' Petula says as she beats down the duvet around her back with her arm so no cold can get in.

'The bouncer says he's not closed to the idea, but I might need to give him a push in the right direction.' She has her left arm up above her and is leaning on it.

'Although he's quite adventurous, you know, like that. I might get him a bit pissed at the weekend and see if he's up for it. See how far I can push him. I've got that pink thing I told you about under the bed. I'll give it a quick wash in the bath tomorrow. He doesn't have to know it's been used before, does he?' Petula laughs, then turns onto her back and I can tell she is in love again and waiting for my reaction, which I don't feel like giving her. I am on my back looking at the ceiling, failing to read the romance novel I have in my hands which I took from Mum's house. It's called *Doctor on Call* but, from the book cover where a painted nurse in the background seems to be wistfully but with a hint of sex dreaming of the doctor in the foreground, should really be called *Nurse on Heat*. I'm still on the first paragraph. I'm reading it over and over again but the words are meaningless, although it's comforting to hold it as I know that she'll have read it, have held onto it, knowing that she believes in some form of love, even though it's the sort where you have to let the man be all man.

It's my first day back at work tomorrow since all the trouble in Brighton and Petula has stayed with me every night since we've been back. She is making it obvious that she thinks I need looking after and keeps alluding to a chat she had with the nurse before we left the hospital. She has told me she thinks I am a bit mentally disturbed at the moment and has removed the sharp bread knife with the perforated edge from my drawer, the toilet bleach has vanished and the washing-up liquid is now pre-mixed ready to go with water and it's difficult to get bubbles. She has taken the spare key to my flat and has popped in every night immediately after work, and each time looks relieved, while pretending she hasn't really noticed, to find me on the sofa watching the news in my dressing gown and not on the floor with my mouth open with blood draining out of the side.

I don't feel that bad. I'm just not peckish, which probably means I am not quite myself. I keep thinking about all the things I won't know about you and never can, unless Mum comes back and I ask her, but I don't know how much she'd be willing to give away. And then I think what do I know about you? Apart from you dying a long time ago and leaving Mum to look after us as best as she could and by that I mean not very well, not compared to the other children with their tightly packed lunches and hugs outside the school gate.

'Well, goodnight then.' Petula yawns.

I give up on Mum's romance book and throw it down next to me, then turn out the light. I'm still not used to Petula sleeping with me, it all feels a little odd, a bit overdramatic. If I'm likely to do something stupid, as she puts it, it wouldn't be when I'm in bed or at night. I mean, there is plenty of time in the day when she's at work to swallow pills or hang myself with a rope from the light fitting. But you see, I don't even want to commit suicide, she has got that quite wrong. I know what will make everything all right. I'm going to find Simon and meet somebody else; I'm not sure about Mum. Those are the only things which will get me out of this situation, not dying. And I don't mind if, with that some-body else, we just fall in love only a little this time, maybe the distance from the edge of my bed to the carpet if you can measure it. I don't want that diving-off-a-skyscraper-with-no-parachute-type of love any more.

Petula has suggested I look for love on the Internet as she says that that is where love is easily found these days and I have agreed to it and am planning to go to the Internet café to open an account and while I'm there I'm going to post that photo of Simon/Amanda off to the Missing Persons website. I'm going to use that photo I took just before Christmas when he was trying out a new look based on his current obsession with Uma Thurman in the film *Pulp Fiction*. That is who he said Amanda most looks like. I had to agree as I had never met Amanda properly before, only glimpsed small experiments and not a whole being. He came into my room wearing a white fitted shirt which was semi-transparent so I could see his white padded bra tucked into a pair of black capri pants. His black bob glistened and he had done his make-up immaculately. It felt difficult at first as I watched Amanda nervously cross her legs on the bed and hold a mug of coffee, as my brother was still so apparently sitting there with his hands around the mug. But this time I noticed there was something else in his eyes, as if the way I looked at him would make him feel like he/she had succeeded or not. I was suddenly Amanda's mirror and her judge. I tried to imagine we were meeting for the first time and we started to chat about what sort of shoes she liked. After a while he said, 'It's still me, you know, you don't have to pretend you haven't met me before, you idiot,' and that made me relax a little and that's when he asked me to take his photo and it was only when he smiled and I looked through the camera lens, twisted the lens to focus on her face, until the two half-moons in the centre of the focus matched, until the view frame glistened with clarity, that I could see that this was how it was going to be from now on, how she was.

Internet dating is all the rage and is not seen as being desperate any more, Petula says, even if you are popular and go out regularly to bars you can do it as long as you don't take it too seriously.

I know I am still in love with Sally, whatever that means, but she hasn't bothered to find out if I am dead or alive, unless she rang the hospital and asked and they didn't inform me. Even so, the point is she never wanted me to know whether she had rung or not, so that means she wants me to realise that she just doesn't care. With this new Internet dating thing, I reckon if I meet someone just as good as her I might be able to forget about her. Even if it was only for a few minutes it would be worth it.

That's settled, then, and I can go to sleep now. Petula has put on her black eye mask she got from off a plane and has already gone to sleep silently on her side. She isn't a bad bed guest as she doesn't make a murmur. Yesterday she said she doesn't dream. I said I didn't believe her and she replied that that was why her life was so eventful, to make up for the lack of it when she was asleep.

My dreams are never eventful. They are often just me in our old house in my old room with a sense that you are there and everything and everyone is in place, worrying because I have forgotten to revise for my imminent exams.

31

Ruby has bought me a new half-apron. It has yellow roses on it and a frill around the edge and ties up at the back with a pink bow. It's meant to cheer me up and it does in a Doris Day kind of way. The regulars have signed a card, the front of which shows some bears holding up drinks in the air under a banner saying Welcome Back. I have only been off for a few days. It's the caff's way of acknowledging that something's gone on without actually mentioning it.

Ruby asks me how I am feeling as I put my jacket in a carrier bag. Her mascaraed eyes are blinking and I think about the way she perfectly coats the eyelashes beneath, wishing I could get it that right.

'Much better, thanks,' I say and she nods towards the table to sit down.

She makes me a mug of tea and she takes out her cigarettes, easing herself down to sit with me.

'I was worried, you know, love,' she says, lighting up and inhaling. This is her one cigarette she has before the customers arrive. Her lipstick is on the end of the brown filter tip as she pulls it away from her mouth.

'You know you can always come to me, whatever it is, you know. I've seen you grow up, remember. I've seen your family grow up and change and I'll always try to be there for you, as much as I can. You don't need to hold it all in, you know it's not good for you, it can make you ill, give you cancer, weaken your heart. I mean, I know Petula can be as daft as a brush when it comes to men, but she really does care. We both do. I think you frightened her, disappearing and being in that hospital. I know you did me.'

She reaches across to my arm and rests her fag-free hand on it. She has her old wedding ring on. I've never noticed that she still wears it.

'I know, Ruby. But I really am much better now.' I look at the black dots of tea which have escaped from the tea bag. I don't want to appear emotional on my first day back and her kindness will bring it all up if she keeps on. I want to seem normal again like I used to be before I had to start thinking about what normal was. Sensing that I am not going to open up, she tells me the news of the last few days and it is strange how nothing goes on in the caff until you are away.

'Now what's been happening since you've been gone? Ah yes, well, the most important thing is that I think Cyril's mind might be going a bit as he turned up in his slippers without his coat on the other morning. It's lucky it wasn't raining, but it was too cold to be without a coat. We're going to have to keep an eye on him, check he's washing and eating plenty of broccoli. They say it's good for the memory. I said to him, "Where are your shoes, Cyril?" and he said they were on his feet and when I made him look at them he seemed bewildered, as if I had put the slippers there myself. It's such a shame, isn't it? But we'll all rally round. He's been coming in for what now?' And she pauses as she counts years in her mind. 'Thirty years now, since we opened the caff. God, all that time . . . all those fried eggs.' And she laughs and I see mountains of eggs on toast.

'Now, on a more cheerful note, Alf has come back from Thailand with the news that he's marrying a bride half his age. He said he was introduced to her by his son on the Internet and that they both like beer and going for walks so he thinks it will work, and I suppose it will as what more do you need at his age apart from a little company on a spring evening? I don't expect she's got much either. She's arriving next week and we are all invited to the ceremony. I said he could have the reception do here as I know it'll only be his son and a few of us. We can decorate the caff and do the food and he'll get in the drink. What do you think? I thought we could have Thai green curry to make his wife feel welcome. Spring rolls would be good too but I'm not sure if they are too Chinesey.' She is drawing spring rolls in oval shapes on the plastic tablecloth. 'Nevertheless, I'm sure she'll be pleased. Now you, as long as you are all right to start work again, let's get started and get those potatoes peeled. It's fish pie today.' And she stands, picking up the ashtray, and I follow her to the counter to get my new apron on and she ties it for me and I feel glad to be back.

She doesn't mention the conversation she and Petula had had in the caff when we got back from Brighton and neither does Petula, but I know they had one as Petula had disappeared for an hour, bringing back only a loaf of bread and a pint of milk, and Ruby had rung and told me not to come in until the following Saturday, which is today.

The caff is busy and everyone is talking about the whale that's got stuck up the Thames. Every hour the whale is on the radio and there is a buzz in the caff; it's good to have news that isn't to do with a war or another murder. According to the news bulletin the whale is by Battersea Bridge now and Mary and Hilda have decided to get the train up to go and see it and Cyril joins in after a little deliberation. He is muttering to them about the day he caught a huge fish in the park pond when he was a boy and how it was nearly the size of a whale and it bent his rod, but they do not listen as they get up, clasping their purses in their hands and their handbags to their breasts, as if ready for battle. They tell him to get his coat on and use the toilet before they go, which he does and he comes out with a little dribble down the front of his trousers and Ruby has to tell him to do his zip up. He bumbles behind them as they leave, continuing with his fish story. It is quite an event, everyone agrees, and it gives the air of an unusual holiday to the day.

By three o'clock Ruby says the takings are definitely down. The whale up the Thames has made the day a lot quieter than it would normally be. By five o'clock the caff is empty and has been since Elsie left; Ruby decides to shut up shop early. I wipe down all the plastic tablecloths with warm soapy water and collect the salt and pepper pots and the ketchup bottles with a tray and leave them on the counter. Ruby cashes up and finds a fake one-pound coin. She says she'll use it in the big supermarket up the road when she gets her lottery tickets. Picking up the chips first and any other large bits, I then stack all the chairs onto the tables and mop around them. The radio plays classical music and I swing the mop with the motion of the music, twisting it back in the bucket to rinse the dirty water out when it gets to the dramatic part.

We do this every day and I am glad of it, although the music is not always the same. There is a great satisfaction about getting the caff ready for the next day through placing the objects needed in the correct place. Some would find this boring, but it reminds me of what I found on the small piece of paper in my fortune cookie the other day from the takeaway: 'May you live in interesting times – *Chinese curse*'.

It hints that it is far better when nothing much happens, which I agree with of late.

I have bagged up the tea cloths and the hand towel from the toilet and will drop them into the dry-cleaner's on the way home, as is done at the end of every Saturday. Then we get our coats on and turn off the lights, making sure the appliances are turned off, apart from the fridge which glows all night. I say goodbye to Ruby as she turns the key to lock up the caff, pushing at the door twice to make sure it is really locked.

Petula has invited me down to dinner tonight. She says she needs to practise a recipe she wants to try on the bouncer when he comes to visit her, and also the meal is intended as a celebration for me feeling normal again, which we both assume is true since I am back to work. She has bought a whole fish, a rainbow trout, and I am a little dubious about it as it's something neither one of us has attempted to cook before, plus it seems at odds with the day and the whale story. They are still trying to save it.

A little after eight, I come downstairs to return her toothbrush and her eye mask. Her watch over me is officially over and I have my bed back to myself. A little later the fish arrives out of the oven and the fish's eye stares at her as she cuts it open and Petula grimaces and puts a serviette over its head. We are downstairs in her flat at the oval kitchen table and she has tried to make the table look as if we have gone out to that Spanish bistro up the road. In the wine glasses are white serviettes folded into fans so the tops fall open like the tails of peacocks and there is a candle stuck in the neck of an old bottle which she says she wants to trickle down the side and set. There are two sets of knives and forks and a spoon across at the top. We even have side plates. She told me I was to dress up and be down for eight. I am wearing a silver vest top made from stretchy sequins which doesn't make my arms look too wide and a black skirt with 'Barely Black' tights. It is to be 'the dinner which marks the start of the rest of your life', as she put it.

As I sit at the table I am reminded of what it felt like when it was my birthday, when everything about the day was about me, but the fish is too salty and the wine too red and there is that great absence still. But I don't say anything as Petula looks so pleased. She said earlier that 'buying a whole fish really means that I am growing up and yet still not afraid of experimenting'. She has only eaten a little when she looks up and swears, stabbing the table with the blunt end of her knife.

'Bugger.'

'What?' I say, jumping a little.

I watch her get up and go to the fridge, yanking open the door.

'I forgot the starters.' She pulls out two plates from the fridge and then slams the door shut with her foot and presents two halves of avocado filled with prawns in a seafood sauce. The sauce is the unnatural colour that, as children, we used to paint skin.

'The whole meal was to have a fish theme.' Her eyes flash across the room and she gets the plates and before I can suggest we have them now she has scraped the starters into the bin with her fingers. The pedal-bin lid drops down.

'It's ruined. I'll have to write it all down so I don't forget the order of things when he comes. Perhaps you could ring down and remind me I've made starters before I start? I'm not used to having three courses, but I really want to impress him as he says he's a really experimental cook and can judge a woman's personality by the way she is in the kitchen. I'm not sure what he meant by that but I'll probably go to pieces in front of him, him watching me from behind as I pull the fish out from the oven, or pour the wine all over him. Him just watching, taking notes about my performance.'

'I'm sure he won't be just watching that,' I say, knowing she'll wear a top which flashes her bra straps.

She sits down heavily in her seat at the table and pours more wine into her glass. She pushes her plate away from her and then only gives me a splash into my glass and I think how strange the bouncer sounds and wonder whether he is like Elsie, but reads food instead of tea.

Petula has bought a bottle of red wine that comes from South Africa. It says on the back that the breeze from the ocean mixes with the grape to create its full-bodied texture. She said to me before the meal that she wasn't allowing me to drink too much at the moment, considering my state of mind as a hangover could set me back weeks, but I don't care as I've never liked red wine. There is a four-pack of Guinness in the fridge to help my blood get better if I want them.

'Don't worry,' I say. 'You'll get it right. Maybe I could be the waitress?' I laugh, trying to lift her out of herself and then there is that usual gap where I start to shift about in my seat as her mood has cancelled out any feeling of optimism there was before the meal and I can't think what to say. And before I know it, so that her mood will alter back to the one she was in before she forgot the starters, I have asked her about the only subject I know she will like.

'How is the bouncer then? Have you heard from him lately?'

'Oh yes.' She perks up right away. 'He texted just before you came down.'

She looks for her phone and sees it charging on the side.

'He has sent me one hundred and forty-two texts since I met him, you know, which was only eight days ago. I looked at the total on the bus the other day; it works out at about eighteen a day. You know, I've not replied to all of them. That's how you keep them interested. Or at least keep them waiting for an hour or two to make them wonder what you are doing. He's waiting for a reply at the moment and I didn't tell him who I was making dinner for; I just casually mentioned I had someone coming round.'

'You mean you are playing a game,' I say, thinking aloud and about how I hadn't tried to suppress anything with Sally.

'No, silly. Not lie, but don't say it all in one go. Choose your words carefully. Keep them on a bit of string. Sometimes don't put an x at the end. It drives them mad, well, apart from Ewan who was a rule unto himself but I put that down to his artistic-ness . . .'

Then it hits me, maybe that's where I went wrong. I don't know how or when Petula learnt that to keep someone waiting was to keep them around; maybe it's from one of the women's magazines or from the saying 'treat them mean keep them keen' which was said at school a lot about boys. Or maybe from all the soap operas or films where the characters agonise over the phone while trying to conduct their daily lives as if they don't care but keep looking at the phone, as if it doesn't matter to them that someone else is deciding their fate.

But, if you think about it, there is always a risk that if you keep someone waiting too long, they will get bored and go off. How do you know what is an appropriate amount of time anyway? A day to me would seem like a week, and a few days to Petula might be just like my one day, but someone who has never been kissed before surely would only be able to stand a few minutes before wanting that call/text/flowers.

Now I realise that's why Sally went, because she was bored, because I couldn't wait to keep her waiting. I let her know how I felt as soon as I felt it and that is not exciting or mysterious enough.

How much like an old-fashioned dance this whole courting thing is, one step back and they follow forward, one step forward and they step back. Too many steps in the wrong direction and you've lost your dancing partner forever.

But upstairs, in my flat, there is Kate's number on the board winning triumphantly over the bathroom fluff and the pubes. Tomorrow, Petula and I are going to take a picture of me in the park with her digital camera for what is called my profile for the Internet dating agency. I said I would like some natural ones of me feeding the ducks and wandering beside the early daffodils as they are cheery and will show that I am normal and have an outside kind of lifestyle, even though I don't. Petula is going to scan all the best photographs onto a CD at work and I shall pick one.

Pick the one which makes me look as if I am ready for love again and the one which makes my legs look a little longer and slimmer than they really are.

32

I'm sure I saw her go past, I'm sure it was her, out of the caff window. It was her hair, the way she walked with a slight jump in her step, her winter coat flapping back revealing one of her knees. I could have run across the street after her, dodging the people, calling out her name, and finally caught up with her and touched her on the shoulder forcing her to turn round, but I didn't. My mind had already raced ahead and convinced itself that it couldn't possibly be her and that the person who turned round wouldn't have had her eyes. It would be some-body else's confused face replacing the face I want to see, like a bad impressionist.

Maybe I am scared, in case the daydream of the reunion never happens. In case there is a stony silence and she just looks through me as if I never existed. As if all those moments we shared had never taken place and there is nothing left but wishy-washy recol-lections of unsure memories. Perhaps I am just worrying that she will never come home, that she, our mum, your old wife, has gone forever and Simon will never be found and that will be it, this will be my life.

Now the fine lines around Sally's eyes are an all too distant memory and I can't clearly recall the way her neck arched down onto her shoulder, I am thinking about Mum and where she is and whether she is on a boat wearing her floppy sun hat, laughing and chinking glasses with sailors and how it didn't seem to matter so much when I had Sally, or was consumed with the heartbreak, how Mum didn't seem to matter so much.

The woman has disappeared up the road behind the plumbing

shop and I go back to the counter and tap my finger on the top.
There are seven jam doughnuts piled up on a stand under a plastic
lid to keep them fresh and there are seven customers in the caff.
There is a fine balance about the number of doughnuts to people
and it would be even finer if each of them ordered one.

A mother with bleached hair and dirty roots has sat down with
her son beside Elsie's table. They make up two of our seven
customers. The boy is about eight and is in his school uniform and
he looks pale and grey, matching the collar of his white school
shirt. They may have just come from the doctor's surgery. We get
a lot of trade from the doctor's. The mother is smoking, reading
the front of a newspaper whose headline says 'WHALE DEAD', and
is letting the smoke drift over and go in her son's face. The whale
dying has been news all day and the radio is blaming the govern-
ment for putting out satellite signals which confused the whale
into going the wrong way. Cyril seems upset and unsettled because
he saw it dying, he said there wasn't much point in living any more
when you've seen something like that die. We give him a free
doughnut with his tea.

I go over and smile at the boy and ask him what would he like.
He looks up at his mother as if to say what could he have and the
mother waves her cigarette and says, 'Have what you like.'

'Ice-cream soda then,' he says, his eyes all wide.

'No, have a Coke,' the mum says.

'But you said I could have what I like.'

And the mother turns her face to the child and says in a very
low pointed voice, 'Don't you dare argue with me. Did you hear
what I said? I said have a Coke.'

The boy says nothing now but looks like he is going to cry.

'What will it be then?' I say.

'Two Cokes,' says the mother.

I'm not sure whether it's a money issue, since the ice-cream
sodas are three times the price of a Coke, or maybe she just likes
making him feel small. Whichever way, she knows she can do what

she likes as she is the one with the cash. I want to make him his drink, the one he wants. I want to hold him and slap her. Pinch her so she realises what she is doing.

So I get out the ice cream, without asking Ruby first, and pour out a glass of lemonade, then with the scoop I plop two lumps of ice cream into it so it fizzes and spits. I take it over to the boy, who at the sight of it sits up, all eyes on the drink, then me and then his mother. He waits nervously as she raises her head from the paper.

'It's on the house,' I say and the boy relaxes and puts the long spoon from off the saucer into the glass and the mother says, looking up at me suspiciously, in a voice which I know is more polite than her real one, 'Oh. Well. Say thank you then, to the lady.'

'Thank you,' the boy says, not knowing how much on his side I am.

'You're welcome,' I say and as I walk away I hear her say to him in a hushed tone, 'You're lucky, you got your own fuckin' way this time. Don't think it'll always happen.'

And I turn back and I can see his head down eating his ice-cream soda, pretending what she is saying doesn't hurt, his small ear tuned in to receive her nasty comment, and now I know why I am telling you about this because it reminds me of the time Mum caught Simon in her slip and she slapped him on his leg. She raised her hand high and let it swing down and her hot hand-print was left on his leg. The shape of the hand burnt through the silk slip and after she had slammed herself shut in her bedroom, he hitched up the slip, taking it off and looked at what remained. He put his hand on top of her handprint. You could still see the ends of her fingers red and raw extending from beneath his, as they were much longer. He folded up the silk slip and left it outside her door and we all returned to sit in our rooms until we heard her door open again.

33

'Looking for love' is the only thing I've written under the picture on my profile. It seems right to be honest from the start and say exactly what I am after as it might make it happen more quickly. Then I can place my entire recent trauma in a box which I can throw into the canal alongside the dead characters of soap operas, avoiding the ducks' heads.

The Internet dating agency is called 'New Horizons' and has a picture of two women holding cocktails on a white sandy beach at sunset, dressed in white flappy trousers. I presume it is sunset and not sunrise as otherwise the website would be one for people who are searching for love who have a drink problem. In my photo, I am underneath a blue spotted umbrella, because it was raining that day we went to the park, and I'm holding it slightly behind me so the light through the umbrella doesn't make my face look blue. The daffodil heads are drooping downwards under the weight of the pelting rain but I am standing tall and proud as I imagine I have a broom handle up the back of my coat. Before going out, Petula, 'being a friend' as she'd put it, had insisted on doing my make-up, but had made me look orange, so I wiped off most of it in the toilet by the pond. I am grinning, showing my teeth and I think I look like Mum did when she was my age, although I'm a little more plump.

I haven't written anything else under my hobbies or favourite travel destination as I can't help but think that it doesn't make sense to describe yourself by what film star you like or where you've been to on a plane, even if I had been on a plane. What does that have to do with the essence of someone? After reading some of the profiles I realise that some people are completely the other way and too wildly specific about what and who they are looking for; they want to meet someone to eat oranges with in Seville who isn't too needy but is comfortable in their own skin, or to go hiking in Peru with someone who is a free spirit and into reiki, or they're just looking for a well-balanced busty Leo who will rid them of their Cancerian shyness.

Every single person seems to like red wine, long walks and the cinema.

So, I am not putting a thing, as I think someone will just see me and know that I am the one for them, like I did with Sally.

It's been three days now and I haven't had one message. My profile has been looked at by thirty-two people and still there are no messages. I guess it will take some time so I have decided to call Kate, the student. I kept looking at the piece of paper on the pinboard and taking it down, reading the number and then pinning it back, not sure if it is the right thing to do. But now it is in my pocket as I walk towards Mum's house and my fingers are warming the piece of paper.

There was a red-and-black butterfly on the bus on the way up here, a peacock. It flew across and landed on the ledge right in front of me. Its leg began to stroke the window alongside, trying to get out, its two sets of eyes on its wings spying me. I should have cupped it in my hand and let it go, but I was afraid to. Afraid it might be too disorientated if I'd done that. As well, I didn't know if the bus ride was the right thing for it, as the bus might have been playing an important role in the butterfly's destiny and if I intervened I might change its fortune forever. And then for some reason I think of Sally and how easily it all happened between us and how even easier it was to all go wrong and how contrived it feels to call Kate, as if I am forcing love to appear.

Just before my stop, the butterfly was flapping at the window and it struck me that it could have flown straight out of my stomach, it was that unusual to see one on the bus.

In the end, mobile in sweaty hand, I dial the number and hold my breath and press the green button on the phone and it says 'Calling . . .' and the number blinks as it tries to connect and I think of the signal bouncing off the satellite in space and heading down to Brighton. After three complete rings, she picks up her mobile and it rustles for a while before she speaks as if it is in her pocket or at the bottom of her bag. I can hear Brighton and the wind blowing down her phone and it makes my stomach lurch as I remember the Sea View Hotel and the revelation of the non-existent baby.

'Hello. Hello, who's that?' she says and it's her voice in my ear, talking to me.

'Hello, Kate, it's me,' I say, and there is a pause and I hear a car drive past and some women's voices.

'I met you the other weekend in the drag bar. Do you remember? You looked after my coat and we walked to a party and you gave me this number to call you. Do you remember that?' I say, realising this is the first time I have made a call like this and I feel desperate and exposed and like I am not taking in enough air, I am forgetting to breathe.

And then there is a pause and she says, 'Oh yes! What a surprise,' and begins to talk and says she is having a stroll along the seafront to get over a hangover from the night before at the student union. I ask her how college is going and she says it is good and then there is another pause and I take in a deep breath and ask her if she wants to come up to London one day soon and that we could go on the London Eye (the London Eye thought was spontaneous). She hesitates and I take it suddenly as rejection and feel foolish and think I should hang up and as I take the phone away from my ear, I can hear her miniature voice replying, saying she would love to and asking when. I put the phone back to my ear.

'My day off is a Sunday,' I blurt out, stilted, as if I'm a foreign student learning to speak English, and she says, 'Good,' again, 'maybe this Sunday then?' and we agree to meet by the London

Eye at one o'clock in the afternoon. The phone call ends gawkily, neither one of us knowing how to finish and when the second goodbye has been said and I've hung up I take in a deep breath and feel fingers play the harp in my stomach. Out of the blue, I have something to look forward to and it doesn't matter that I made it happen, in fact it's all the better for it.

By the time I arrive at Mum's house I realise that I can't recall the walk there, as my conversation on the mobile to Kate replaced the normal observations en route and it is as if I have just suddenly arrived and not journeyed there at all. I didn't get to notice the new pink blossom on the branches or the twisted lager tins in the kerb, like I normally would have. I might have trodden in dogshit and I still wouldn't have noticed.

Mum's gate is open and it stops me, as I sense there is something different.

The gate is never normally open, it is always closed. People know to close it. As I walk across the crazy paving to the porch, I am not really expecting to see the outline of her, but it is suddenly there, through the frosted pane in the front door I can see her in the kitchen, standing still; maybe looking through her post. We haven't spoken since that Christmas Day when Simon stormed out and later I did the same and I turned up at Petula's with my rucksack and nowhere to go. The last time I saw her she was sat motionless in your chair with the television on too quiet to hear it. She wouldn't talk and she wouldn't look at me. Our presents were still under the tree all wrapped up. I still don't know what she got me. The last sentence I said to her was 'This is ridiculous', and she didn't flinch. If only she had shouted or made an animal noise or anything, anything was better than one of her silences.

There is a shadow which moves into the kitchen and it's a man, a tall man with dark hair like yours was and I almost think it could be you. Their shadows merge and I can see that they are standing closely together with their arms around each other and possibly kissing. I step back as I don't want to see her kissing a man I don't know, or any man for that matter. I don't want to know that they might be using their tongues as he puts his hand in her bra and she unzips his trousers and lowers her body down and I know I shouldn't be saying this, especially to you, but at this specific moment in time, I wish her dead. And then all the rage comes to my cheeks and I have the key out of my pocket and it's twisting in the lock. I'm going to tell her what I think of her and how she was so unlike a mother and how she's driven Simon away and destroyed the little of what's left of our family and how could she and why would she? I'm going to tell her that she made us feel like she didn't love us, in fact that we aren't loved and that's why we are flailing around, looking for whatever we can find and can't find it because it doesn't exist, because it is what we should have been, all together, a unit or a flock.

The door opens and I struggle to get the key out, so momentarily my back is to the kitchen and I hear, 'Excuse me. What do you think you are doing?' coming from the man in the kitchen and I turn round to go to blast off at Mum but she isn't there. The woman who is is nothing like her, in fact she is half Mum's age and a redhead.

'Where's Mum?' I say.

'Who?' he says.

'She lives here, this is our house. I'm her daughter.'

To the right of me I see boxes, cardboard boxes stacked in the lounge with red arrows pointing upwards to say which way up they should stand. They are on our beige carpet, which remains there with the wallpaper on the walls, but the painting of the yellow meadow behind the country gate has gone and the one of the olde-worlde children playing with the King Charles spaniel too. Only the picture hooks are left.

'We've just rented it, we only moved in yesterday,' the redhead says, walking up the hall towards me with what I think might be an Irish accent. 'Didn't your mother tell you?' Her eyes look bemused.

'No, no she didn't mention it.'

'Well, we've rented it through that agency on the high street. You know the one opposite the police station,' she says, moving her finger, drawing the connection between the two in the air.

'How long for?' I ask.

'Well, until we find our own place and get everything sorted. We've leased it for six months,' she says.

'Six months? Are you sure? I mean, are you sure you have the right address? I was here only the other day and Mum's stuff was still there, in her room, her old prescriptions were in the bathroom cabinet. Maybe . . . can I have a look upstairs?' I say. I want to know what's left. It was only the other day I was sat on Mum's bed with her love book in my hand.

'Well, I'd rather you . . .' she begins to say, looking at the man, but he reads her mind and says, 'It's OK. I'll take her up there.'

And before I know it, I am being escorted up our stairs onto our old landing outside our rooms and he is blocking me but I can tell not wanting to enter the rooms either with me. He knows it would feel like he was intruding. After a moment's hesitation, I walk past him and push open Mum's bedroom door and there are unfamiliar hard new-looking silver suitcases next to the bed and a duvet pulled back where they have obviously slept the night before. The cover is all browns and creams and creates a trio of ice-cream colours with Mum's pink walls.

Simon's room has been painted in cream magnolia and mine the same. They smell of fresh paint and apart from the two single beds, which have on clear mattress protectors, all the furniture has been removed.

'You see, we weren't lying. She's not here. We're not squatters.' The man laughs and I ignore him and I have an urge to look in the airing cupboard where I used to find Simon sometimes crouched in the dark, all snug next to the boiler.

'Maybe you should go and see the people at the agency and

they might be able to give you some information,' he says behind me, on the landing.

'Yes, I think I suppose I'll do that,' I say.

I walk back down the stairs and the woman has her hand on the end of the banister. She has cold blue eyes which I notice are red around the edges, like she's been crying, and as I walk past her I stop momentarily and stand in our hallway, aware that the bookcase, which doubled up as a shelf for the telephone, has gone, a new-looking phone with its messy unravelled cord sits on the box on the floor instead.

'Did my mother leave a forwarding address for her post?' I turn to her and she says no, shaking her head, and looks again at the man who is stood on the bottom step of the stairs with his arm not so casually blocking the entrance to upstairs.

'I'm sorry to have disturbed you,' I say at the front door, my keys still hanging from the lock. My hand starts to pull at them but they won't budge, the lock always was a bit tricky.

'Um, excuse me,' the redhead says, forcing me to look back at her blotchy face. 'I think it might be right that you leave the front-door key with us. I mean, you have no use for it at the moment, do you? And when we leave we will hand it back to the agency and they can pass it on to you. You know, it's a security thing, isn't it. I need to know who has a key and who doesn't. This is our home for the time being and we should be the only one with keys. I'll have to have a word with the agency.' The key releases itself from the lock and I feel the groove of it between my fingers, its specific markings a match for this unique lock.

'It's my key,' I say, looking at the set, which includes the keys to my flat, the caff and Petula's spare.

'Yes, but you don't need it while we live here, do you?' she says, her voice beginning to get an edge to it.

'But it's mine. This is my family home,' I say, slightly pleading with her, and then she puts out her hand, firmly and flatly towards me.

'Look, you shouldn't have one to this house at the moment, now it's been rented out, should you?' She holds out her hand further and I clench my hand around the set.

'Please can you give it to me, now? Or we'll change the locks,' she says and I realise that I have no choice as Mum's not here and she's getting more het up about it than I think is normal. I have to take nearly all the keys off of the silver band to get to the one I need and it hurts my thumb as the two metal rings are so tightly bonded that to prise them apart you have to wedge it between them and then slide the keys out. It takes some time and the woman tries to help me but her fingers get in the way. When I've finally twisted it out, I hand her the key and she says she is sorry to have shouted, but it's been a very emotional time because they were made homeless after their house caught fire and they've lost nearly everything and could only salvage a few books and bits and bobs from the back room, which was largely untouched but the smell of smoke gets everywhere, doesn't it, it gets right under your skin.

And then she glances across at the man who looks away and says, 'You may have read about it in the local newspaper. We lost our baby in it. It was on the front page.'

'No, I didn't see it. I'm so sorry,' I say, and I really am and I see in her eyes an immeasurable grief. She walks off back to the kitchen clutching herself in her own arms, her head lowered, and I leave and he shuts the door behind me and I hear the sound, the clunk of the door. And it's only then I realise that the sound of that door used to be so unimportant when I went out, as I never noticed it, but that's the thing, I was always just going out and never really leaving, unlike today.

When I glance back through the frosted glass of the front door, I can see them standing in the kitchen in the same way as when I first saw them. Now, I see them as they are, two strangers' shadows holding on to one another.

The bus takes me away and I look for the peacock butterfly.

There is no nature on the bus and even if there was I am too distracted by the smell. The man in front is giving off that suffocating tramp smell and it has filled the lower deck. It makes me hold my nose and breathe through my mouth, but I am concerned that I am still breathing in his odour and that it will taint my breath. On the shoulders and back of his jacket is a heavy dusting of dandruff and his hair hangs limp but matted above his collar where he has slept. He is talking out loud and seems perturbed and I try to see if he has one of those wire microphone things which dangles from the ear so that you can talk without having to hold on to your mobile. You see people in the street chatting away to this wire, busy in conversation although it sounds like a monologue, often appearing crazy until you spot the wire. The wire is evidence that they are not insane. But of course he hasn't got a mobile. He wouldn't have one because he is considered mad and mad people like him cannot afford mobiles. He wouldn't need one anyway as he has all the conversations he likes with himself.

I am relieved to get off the bus to be able to inhale a chest full of air through my nose again and the air seems magnificent, although slightly fumed from the bus.

The estate agent's has a rubber plant by the door which shakes as I enter. There is a young woman on the front desk with large gold hooped earrings who is on the phone and she glimpses up at me with a look on her face, slightly annoyed, as if I am intruding. She has a cactus plant next to her computer and I stand to the side of her desk waiting for her to finish her call. There are two tidied desks behind her where no one is seated.

'Yeah, look, I've got to go. I'll speak to you later then, yeah? OK then, bye,' she says and I guess it might not be a call to do with work, although when she's hung up, she takes ages to scribble something down on a yellow sticky pad, delaying the moment she has to acknowledge me.

'Yes, can I help you?' she finally says, sitting up in her chair with her pen in between her fingers like a cigarette, beckoning for me to take a seat. She has a strong south London accent and I feel uncomfortable as I think I recognise her as one of the naughty girls from my old secondary school.

'Well, yes, maybe,' I say. 'Look, this is a little difficult. I have just been round to my old house, where I grew up, expecting to find that nothing had changed and maybe my Mum had come home from her travels but to my great surprise my mother seems to have rented it out, without my knowledge, and the people there said that they are leasing the house through this agency. So, I was wondering if you could give me any clue as to my mum's whereabouts so I can contact her?'

'What? So, you want to know how to rent out a house?' she asks, her eyes dazed, looking out of the window to the high street behind me.

'No,' I say slowly. 'I want to know if you can tell me where my mother might be.'

'Why would I know?' she says.

'Because she is renting out our old house through this agency,' I say.

'So, you want to rent out a house?' she says.

'No, look. Number 73 Gordon Road. My mum is renting it out and I don't know where she's gone and I need to find her. Can you help me?' I say.

'Umm, let's see. What number?' She puts her hand onto the mouse of the computer.

'Seventy-three Gordon Road,' I say.

'Seventy-three Gordon Road. Yes, there it is. Rented out this week.'

'I know it is. Is there an address for my mother then, a Mrs Cathy Rodgerson?' I say.

'No, I'm sorry, I can't give out that sort of information,' she says.

'But she's my mum. It is my old house. Can you tell me where she is, please?'

'No, I'm sorry, it's confidential.'

'But I'm her daughter. I really need to speak to her?'

'Well, maybe she doesn't want to be contacted. Look, I'm not allowed to tell anyone anything important and at the end of the day I'm not going to risk my job by giving you information like that. Customer confidentiality is one of our strong points here. It's our business. My hands are tied. You should really take all this up with your mum, you know.' She rolls her pen across her desk, marking the space between us, and her face is set hard.

'Thanks, at the end of the day, as you say, that's a great help.' I yank open the door so hard that it bangs against the wall and I'm a bit embarrassed and yet surprised at my own strength. The girl is watching me and I can see she is tutting with her eyes narrowed as I pull the door shut and walk off. I turn back to give her one of my rare stares, which will tell her what I think of her and her confidentiality, but she's already got the phone wedged into the crook of her neck and is busy dialling.

I buy pasta tubes from the supermarket on the way home. You know, the ones big enough to fill up your throat and stroke the tube that goes down to your stomach if you can manage to swallow them whole. It should be fine if I make them with that cheese sauce.

34

I am standing on the grass by a line of Japanese tourists, all composing not exactly the same photo of the London Eye, but as good as, with tiny silver cameras on thin-sticked tripods. They are taking it in turn to pose with their wives and children on the grass in front of the Eye, the Thames behind them. I am watching a man and a woman stand in front of the camera, side by side, not touching or smiling for the shot. It appears as if the photo is simply a record and it's strange why we are made to feel like we have to smile for the camera and they don't. In fact, once the photo is taken their faces relax and they walk around the back of the camera, looking at their digital image, and then they crack a smile at each other. I feel jealous of their cameras as mine is still at the mender's with no timeframe as to when it might be fixed.

A small Japanese girl has a bright pink coat on with '100% Sugar' written on the back, with '100% Girl' underneath, and I wonder how they can be so sure she is.

The London Eye was built right on the Thames for the millennium and I think it is beautiful now I am up close. It is a slow-moving big wheel, a cool white colour without any garish splashes of the funfair and it has enclosed pods made of glass, instead of the swingy seats. When I cross the bridge into town on the train, I can see it through the window and from a distance it looks flimsy, as if it might unscrew itself and tilt into the river. But now when I'm underneath it, near to a gallery where I think there was once a sliced-up cow in liquid, it looks magnificently solid.

Kate, the date, should be here any minute. I reach inside my bag for my packet of mints and feel the sandwiches I made earlier as I haven't got much money. I made enough for two as she is a student and will probably be grateful. There is a choice of egg mixed with salad cream or tuna. I would normally put onion in with the tuna but haven't today because of the possibility of kissing later, if all goes well. Instead of taking her out for a meal, as I'd kind of implied, I thought we could go to the pub and eat our sandwiches outside, as it's a bright warm afternoon and much cheaper.

There are tourists everywhere and it is as if London has become every country in the world. I got here much earlier than I needed to and bought the tickets as I was worried what we might talk about if we had to hang around. You see, Petula told me, there are two queues, one to buy the tickets and then the other to get on the wheel, and because I don't want there to be any of those painful silences I thought if I already had the tickets it would speed things up a bit.

In the booking hall, there was a recorded message in many foreign languages, which no one seemed to listen to. As I had little else to do or anyone to speak to I paid attention to the announcement, trying to guess the language. It sounded the most lively in French, whatever was being said. I had lined up behind a group of boys. Two of them looked as if they'd grown overnight and hadn't got used to their bodies yet, their skins awkward and unfamiliar, their hormones making the air musty. They had matching acne and fluffy goosey moustaches. I could smell the foreignness on their coats.

The woman at the desk seemed a bit too friendly and as I was buying the tickets, she offered me a London Eye Experience catalogue and so I flicked through it, thinking it was what she wanted me to do. It had the view from it and numbers on buildings telling you what was what and I thought how handy it would come in and how I would be able to impress Kate with my knowledge of London. It wasn't until I tried to walk off with it that I found out the London Eye Experience catalogue wasn't free. Outside, among the pencils, rubbers and postcards on sale, I deliberated over buying myself a London Eye mug, but knew it was a rip-off and they hadn't been very lovingly made.

I killed time by wandering into the backgrounds of other people's photographs and trying to guess the relationships going on in them, and I felt far away from home with all the foreign voices so I stuck to the grass where there was more space.

Kate sees me before I see her and I spot her waving, standing on her tiptoes, beaming over the heads of the Japanese. She isn't the girl I had in my head and I have to look behind me to make sure she is not waving at someone else. At first I think she can't possibly be the girl I'd sat next to in the pub and feel as if I might have been set up, as if a film crew might jump out at any time, as the girl I met before was prettier, taller and didn't have one side of her head shaved as if she'd had an operation.

She kisses me on the cheek and squeezes my arm.

'It's good to see you again,' she says.

'You too,' I say, squirming backwards. 'Did you have a good journey?' I am telling myself to smile even though deep in my stomach it is telling me to leave.

'Yes. It was really good. I'm amazed at why I don't come up to London more. It only takes an hour, you know. It's so quick, but it's the cost, you see. The train's so expensive. There are those buses you can get now though. I might do that next time.'

'Yes, the buses are cheaper,' I say.

She then puts her hand in her bag and says, 'Oh, I've got something for you.' Her eyes are wide as saucers and as brown as mud. 'Put out your hand,' she says.

So I do and she reveals a stick of rock from behind her back and lifts up my hand higher to rest it in my palm. She awaits my response like a dog who knows they've done ever so well and I look at her, smiling one of those smiles which isn't really one. She has a spot on the side of her nose, a whitehead, and I know I will spend all day looking at it even though I will try not to, wishing it away, wishing her to squeeze it and for her skin to be purer, more like Sally's was.

The queue for the London Eye is not as slow as I thought it would be. It's early spring and most people will save this particular outing for a dependable summer's day. But I like the crisp sky full of perfectly formed clouds, as if they've been freshly painted on, and the way I still need a cardigan but don't need a jacket and how it's the first day I've left the flat without thinking about gloves.

Kate and I are over by the entrance to the Eye. We are waiting for one of two men to check our tickets before we enter the main queue. One has a lisp and is soft and friendly and the other is dismissive with a hard gesturing hand, like good cop bad cop. After that, we hang around, until two men with padded black jackets and microphones on the sides of their faces get us to stand with our legs spread and arms out to the side and wave wands over us looking for bombs. Our bags get checked and I am asked if I have anything sharp in my bag and for a moment I worry he's going to take the sandwiches, which I wrapped in foil. This is one of the most secure places I have ever been to.

Only then are we allowed into the final queue. When we get near the front, we watch the Japanese group step into one of the eggs and there is a rush of excitement in my stomach, like just before stepping on a roller coaster. We are stopped there though, making us the front of our group. Everyone is looking around to see who they might have to share the experience with and by glancing behind us I can see we will be sharing our egg with a family. There is a grandma with her daughter and three children. The grandma and the daughter have the same beaky noses and rich-looking wide scarves thrown expertly around their shoulders. When we are allowed through the barrier we are told to walk fast to get on, as the egg is still moving and for a moment my feet don't know where they are. Everyone seems to burst noisily onto the egg and it takes a while for us all to calm down. The grandma sits straight down on the wooden bench in the centre of the pod, holding the jackets of the children who are getting as close to the edge as possible, as if they'd like to fall into the murky Thames. Other tourists swarm in and everyone fights to get a seat, trying to sit down because it is a ride. We stand up, as far away from them as we can, underneath the word 'west' which is the direction in which the front of the egg faces. South is behind us to our left and as we start to move I can see Crystal Palace rising up like a proud lone point of a star. Kate's eyes are wide open and she is grinning at me.

'This is great,' she says, and I have to agree.

As our egg starts to move up, there is no jolt like on the big wheel at the fair, no swing of the ride, and as we become increasingly elevated over London, I feel a sense of relief, as from up here London is more controllable and it is like looking at my A–Z but much better.

Kate and I are holding on to the handrail, our four hands aligned in front of us, clipped around it. The muddy Thames is directly beneath our feet, the glass curving back making you think you are standing on air, walking on water. We can only really judge how high up we are by seeing how small the people on the ground are becoming. I start to feel a little frivolous as we reach the peak of the wheel. I can tell we are at our highest because the pods to either side of us are below us. I look at all four of our hands and make a comment about what sort of duet we would be playing if we were sat at a piano. She moves one and puts it on my arm, laughing a little too loudly, making the family turn towards us and I see the grandma staring. I try to ignore their glances and the fact that the grandma is whispering something to the daughter about us and see that Kate has chewed fingernails. There is something a bit repulsive about chewed fingernails which are so gnawed that they are right down to where the nail lifts off from the skin.

Her hand remains there and I move away, saying, 'Oh look,' pretending I have just spotted Buckingham Palace for the first time, so she has to pull her hand off. I sense that an Italian couple, who have their arms around each other's waists, have their eyes on us too. Her touching me seems too personal and yet you would think a hand on an arm would mean nothing at all and not cause such a reaction.

'Oh yes, I see. It's got that fountain in the middle, hasn't it?' she says, as I try to show her, and I don't think she is seeing it at all.

Pointing and not being able to catch what someone is pointing at must be one of the most repeated acts on here, that and people discussing their vertigo.

Then she puts her hand into her bag and pulls out a disposable camera. She goes up to the Italian couple and asks them to take a picture of us. The man stands forward and says 'OK' and Kate comes behind me and puts her arms around my waist, the way lovers do who have known each other for a long time. I tighten my cheeks into a smile and she pulls me close into her and rests her chin on my shoulder. The man says 'cheeza' in his Italian accent and his girlfriend laughs, so does Kate in my ear and I think I do too, but I can't be sure. I pull away and Kate moves to the other side of the egg and looks into the distance, until she has been gazing for so long at something that I think she may be in a trance, so I go over to her and she looks pleased that I have fallen for her trick and suggests I get in a photo with Big Ben behind me and I say no, but I end up standing with my hand on the rail looking at her camera, too polite not to smile.

As we come down Kate starts to talk about a nightclub she went to the other night where women were dressed up in army wear and there was an older woman dressed up in a Nazi costume who was leading a woman around on a chain connected by nipple clamps. She says she had felt underdressed as a sailor and was scared to go into the toilets after she'd seen women practising weeing standing up and one had asked her if she wanted to learn how to do it. She says all this quite loudly and doesn't seem to notice that the children have moved across and are standing right next to us, or in fact that there is anyone else in the pod but us, as then out of the blue, as I'm still picturing the Nazi and the nipple clamps, she turns to me and tries to kiss me on my lips and I keep mine shut so that she ends up kissing the space above my lips. Initially her mouth was open, her tongue on view as she zoomed in, but soon she closes it and pulls back when she senses I am uncomfortable.

'What's wrong?' she says. 'I thought you liked me?'

'I do.' (I know I am not looking her in the eye.) 'But not here, it's so public,' I say.

When the egg gets back down to street level I am quite relieved to be leaving the contained space we shared with the family, away from the Italian couple and the bird-like grandma and the few other tourists I had tried to ignore, who in turn had tried to ignore us. We walk along the river, with strolling footsteps as there is no rush, past the street entertainers whose job it is to be painted silver and remain still.

We are now sitting by the river on a wooden pub bench that belongs to the sign which says National Film Theatre. Neither of us has ever been here before and it is like we have got off the London Eye and landed in Paris. There are many people in thick-framed glasses and black polo-neck jumpers drinking proper coffee and one man is wearing a beret. The lamps along the river are what I imagine to be next to the Seine. There are light bulbs strung between each lamp which will hopefully illuminate the wide path later into a perfect film set. The lamp posts have fish swimming about the bottom of them with big swollen lips. We are drinking lager as it's the biggest and strongest drink available for the price. It is that French lager which people say changes their personalities from one minute having a good laugh to the next punching someone in the face. But I can't quite see it having the same effect on us if we eat the sandwiches. I have bought the first round and when I walked to the bar I could see large film stills covering the wall that leads through to the cinemas. I saw that pretty blonde French actress holding a shiny black telephone.

It is so like what I imagine Paris to be that I wish I had made a baguette instead of the sandwiches I have taken out, spreading open the foil onto the table. Kate says she is too excited to eat, so I am making my way through them. One of the French-lady impersonators to my left with lipstick on keeps staring coolly across at them and I am tempted to offer her one when Kate goes to the toilet.

Kate is wearing a blue T-shirt with the words 'Disco Freak' on the front in glittery white lettering. It is so warm that she has taken off her denim jacket and is sitting opposite me resting her face on her hand, her foot pressing onto my foot.

'There's all sorts of shit going down in Brighton,' she says. Her cheeks are getting a little pink from the drink.

'Oh yes?' I say.

'Yeah. You know those girls I was sitting with the night we met in that bar. Well, they were one of the first to get married since it's come in. I mean, they've been together for eight years and seemed really happy until they swapped rings and all that and now one of them's moved out and got it together with a traffic warden. I'm sort of friends with both of them and I don't really want to take sides but I feel sorry for the one that's been left, you know?' Then she pauses and says, 'I'd never get married. Relationships always go wrong in the end, don't they?'

She's said it more like a fact than a question and I take another sandwich and think about it and how young she is to be so down on love and I think about it some more and I suppose a lot of them do, but that doesn't stop people getting into them in the first place. I reckon people choose to have relationships because they wish so hard that love can be true and forever and ever and maybe it's all about believing in that wish rather than not.

'But, I would like to be proved wrong. If you get what I mean,' she says looking straight at me, winking with one slow expert eye, and I shift in my seat and put down the sandwich that I am holding, the tuna flakes suddenly sticking in my throat. Winking was my special thing, I thought, and I feel like she has stolen it.

35

There is a letter on the mat when I get back that night. I show Kate into the lounge and I hear her say 'Wow' and I go and sit on the toilet to read it. It has been returned. On the front of the envelope our old address is written in blue biro with Mum's name above it and then someone has crossed through that and written 'unknown' next to it. The letter has been ripped open at the top and then had Sellotape put wonkily over the rip. On the back is an 'if undelivered please return to' address and it is the address which belongs to mine and Petula's shared house number.

I reopen the letter and it is dated a few days before and it says:

To Cathy wherever you are.

You may remember me as being the rather fashionable best friend of your daughter from secondary school who used to hang around with her at your house listening to Whitney Houston and the Carpenters before I went really slim. You may not but whatever as it's with a great *alarm* that I write to you about your daughter who will probably freak if she ever finds out I've done this. But as you know she's not like me and not the freaking kind but lately she's gone quite mad, making up all sorts of fantasies and even ended up in hospital! She's even lost a bit of weight too! But aside from that if there ever was a time that she needed her mum it would be right now.

Now we both know you never really took to being a mum in the way that most other mums do and as I have no idea what it must be like I can't blame you entirely, but you always did think yourself a bit better than my mum, didn't you, with your tassels on your curtains and your nose always in your love books, always making out that you were superior because your husband had died and my dad had just run off. As if being a widow was so much more respectable than being a single mother, and by being a widow that was a good enough excuse to not have to show love to your children. At least my mum loved me, God rest her soul.

Well look, lady, that won't wash these days, she needs you more than ever because she has found out that she only has six months more to live, a year tops. So you'd better get your act together and look after your dying daughter as I can't all the time as the travel agent's is starting to get busier each day until the end of the summer rush and then there's always the skiing holidays.

You know where we are.

Petula Black

I sit on the toilet and know that Mum's read it and returned it because on the back of the letter, after I have folded it back into three and gone to put it back in the envelope, I notice in capital letters that she has written, **LEAVE ME ALONE**. It's the same pen which has been used on the front of the envelope which says 'unknown'.

36

I woke up with Kate's head in my armpit, her pale arm heavy across my pyjama top. My head is hurting with a pain across one eye, a white stripe staining my vision as if someone has set off a really powerful flashbulb in my face. She is curled into me, awake. I have my arm around her because for that instant before I knew where I was, it wasn't her, the warm body wasn't her, it was just clean comfort.

I take my arm away from her, slightly pushing, forcing her to roll over. I shift so I have my back to her and feel down to the pull-tie ribbon of my pyjamas tight around my waist. It's knotted, cutting me in half, and as I try to release it I look down at the floor and see that a glass of water has fallen over onto the carpet and it is all wet and dark as if someone has mapped out the shape of an alien country. It's all over Mum's *Doctor on Call* book. I lift up the book and shake it; the pages are soggy and stuck together but only the back remains really wet. I place it dripping on the bedside table and pull the duvet up to avoid the sunlight which is illuminating the curtains and this is when I sense Kate is peeping at me. I slump onto my back and let out an obvious sigh, looking at the bobbly ceiling. The sun fades as if on a dimmer switch and the room darkens. She's there, tucked under my duvet, watching. I rub at the pain above my eye and even with my eyes shut I know she is still surveying.

'Good morning,' she says brightly, and her hand is on my thigh moving slowly up and I know where she is trying to go with it. My legs clench together and I know what she wants me to do as she moves closer. She wants me to kiss her, she wants to kiss me, but it all makes me feel repulsed and so instead I blink open my eyes and they cross because her face is so close. I can smell her stale alcohol breath and I guess that I do not fancy her today, and won't in fact any day soon. She is hovering over me, unblinking, like she has been since arriving at the London Eye, and I am concerned that she could be a Martian with no eyelids.

'You've got make-up all under your eyes,' she laughs and she wets her thumb with her tongue and goes to wipe it off. It makes me get up.

'I've got to take some pills. I have an awful headache,' I say.

'I've got a really good cure for a headache,' she says and I pretend I don't hear and go into the bathroom and in the mirror I see my mascara is all under my eyes, making my face look paler than it is. I wash my face in soap and cold water and leave black make-up marks on the towel. I open the medicine cabinet and pop out two tablets from the foil. The water from the pipes is chilled and I take big gulps straight from the tap, feeling the pills vanish down my throat, not worrying about the bathroom-water taste.

Kate has brought her own toothbrush with her and has stuck it in my toothbrush holder alongside my toothbrush on the bathroom sink. I take it out and rest it next to the soap dish, tempted to dip its head into the soap. There are three empty holes once more in my pot. Her toothbrush is sickly pink like the stick of rock.

As I brush my teeth, I remember Petula's letter and try to concentrate on something else by thinking about the pub Kate and I went to, after the South Bank got too cold, and her telling me the pink Hoover story. Although she said she is against gender stereotyping, she spoke for a long time about this Hoover she'd got when she was three and how the attachments were like that of a real grown-up one. I got the impression she thought I would enjoy the story as much as she enjoyed telling it. She then spoke for some length about a project she was doing at art college where she is collecting dust from people's Hoover bags. Unfortunately, although I was listening, I could only stare at the weeping white-head on the side of her nose.

Even though we had drunk for hours and I would normally draw a blank about such an evening, I can still recall the whole night before. I remember the peak of my drunkenness was on the train home when Kate had seemed attractive for the first time that day, because she'd ignored me for a few minutes while she ate her Happy Meal. I watched her bite into a chicken nugget and with the French lager suddenly making her that pretty girl I thought I was going to meet, I swapped seats to sit next to her and kissed her on the cheek while she was still chewing. But it didn't last long and as the train tugged towards home, I started to feel that hungry raw feeling in my stomach where you start to sober up and the moment was lost.

We'd got in and when I came out of the loo, Kate had asked if I had any more alcohol. She put on my CD player and turned up the volume, moving her hips and clicking her fingers to Kylie. I turned it down and thought of Petula lying in bed below with the glow of her mobile lighting up her face as she had sex-text banter with Ivor and the Bouncer, alternating her style and tone for each of their various interests in her, one of which after the bouncer's visit the other day is now 'the beauty of anal sex' as Petula had put it.

We sat up until two, long enough to get her really drunk so she was slurring and unintelligible. I had hoped that she would even-tually pass out but she didn't and she kept on going and talking more and more about her passions which mainly involved the topic of Hoovers and dust. She ranted on about how a life without passion was no life at all. And I suppose I let her because I was avoiding the bedroom part of the evening, pouring her large vodkas and me small ones, knowing she was too drunk to go back to Brighton.

I believe, even though I wasn't exactly attracted to her, I wanted to be wanted by someone and I needed that more than anything. I don't think that is an awful crime, do you? And I thought, well, hoped really, that if Kate squeezed that spot maybe I would fancy her later, perhaps tomorrow I would see her in a different light.

So last night, I let her kiss me, properly, on the front-room carpet. She seemed really into it. But a little too much, as, when we were kissing, her rolling on top of me, pressing down on me, she had started thrashing about and aahing as if in a porn film. And then when we finally went to bed, she had tried to touch me three times, but I kept stopping her hand so in the end I decided it would be much easier for me just to touch her, to keep her from touching me. And when I went to do what Sally had once done to me, she already seemed to be enjoying it too much, before I'd even started she was too loud, too wriggly as if she was amplifying her pleasure like a bad drama student, throwing her voice for an audience or a camera. I remember being to the side of her, looking at her unbelievingly, with just the one hand hovering over her breast, nothing else of me touching her, wondering who she might be doing all this for.

It is half past seven and I have to get going or I will be late for work. She is still in my bed and I thought by the time it took to make the coffee she would have emerged, but she hasn't.

'I really have to go to work,' I say as I push open the door. She turns over towards me, she must have fallen back asleep as her eyes are tiny and stuck together.

'I think I'll just stay here for a while, if that's all right,' she says in a voice younger than hers, a little annoying. And then I spill the coffee I have carried in for her down the front of my dressing gown and walk back into the kitchen with it.

I have a wash and get ready for work and decide to wear all black as her being in my bed is depressing me. I have to keep going in to get my underwear and then my hairspray and then some socks. Each time I enter she is just lying there, unmoved. I do my hair in the kitchen with one ear in the other room and she's still in the bed. My keys are nowhere to be seen and I noisily stack the glasses next to the sink and pick up the loose CDs from the floor. I have to return into the bedroom once more to look for the keys and she has turned over and pulled the duvet around her. After a search in every room, I find them in my coat pocket and decide to drop a heavy hint before I leave. I pop my head around the bedroom door and say could she close the door behind her when she goes.

And as I do she's still in the bed, now semi-upright, planted, smiling with her hands behind her head like it's a bank holiday and she's whistling that Ella Fitzgerald song, 'What a Difference a Day Makes', and I wonder how she would know it but then remember they're using it to advertise instant coffee.

37

By the time I arrive at Ruby's Cafe, a little after eight, it has been transformed with Chinese lanterns, fairy lights and balloons and there are party poppers on each table replacing the sauce bottles. I had forgotten today is the day of Alf's ceremony with the Thai girl, Pim.

'Oh, you've forgotten,' Ruby says looking at my clothes. 'I knew I should have called you to remind you. Lucky I have a spare top with me.' She rummages in her fold-up shopping bag, the one with the Velcro fastening, and pulls out a red Chinese-style silk top with a dragon on the shoulder.

'That'll go with your black trousers you have on and we can put your hair up and threadle through the chopsticks I've got.' She smiles, her eyes shining. She has drawn black eyeliner on top of her eyelids and underneath, giving her Egyptian eyes. I'm sure that Ruby has got it a little wrong with the Chinese clothing and the lanterns. She seems to be treating it more as a fancy dress party than a wedding reception, but it looks festive enough and I'm sure Pim won't notice as she'll probably be too overwhelmed, suddenly transplanted from the palm-fringed beaches of her native homeland, into a caff in south London, married to Alf who has very little but his own teeth.

There is a round cake which Ruby has baked and iced green. She has made small bushes and stuck a bride-and-groom figure under a miniature tree to represent them having a walk in a park. She didn't want to make a traditional white cake as she says that people from that part of the world are used to food full of colour. There is even a little duck pond she has made out of a foil dish.

The groom doesn't have a stick like Alf and the woman looks pale and European with blonde hair, but Ruby says it won't matter as it's just to symbolise their new life together.

The Thai green curry paste makes Ruby choke as she starts to fry it and we have to open the front and back doors of the caff. We are both amazed that the chillies in the paste constrict your windpipe if you inhale it with no windows open. Elsie comes into the caff just in time to help slap Ruby on the back. She is dressed in a robe which I think is an orange flowery dressing gown and after Ruby has had a glass of water Elsie comments on how exciting it is that someone would be able to kill someone with closed windows and Thai curry paste. She has her thin hair brushed back, held with clips and hairspray with two small daffodils pinned to her breast as a corsage and she has painted on her special-occasion aqua-blue eyeshadow and pink lipstick which glistens across her narrow smile.

I am sent to the supermarket with a list before I get changed. Ruby gives me forty pounds from the till. The service starts at eleven at the local registry office and we have a minicab ordered to take us there at ten. I get a mixture of party packs containing spring rolls and bite-size sausage rolls, cocktail sausages and small biscuits called Thai bites and also some mini Scotch eggs, simply because it wouldn't be a party without them. By the time I get back, Alf's son has delivered all the drink and cava for the toast. There are six bottles of sweet white wine and one bottle of red, just in case, and a box of mini French lagers which we put in the stand-up fridge and lemonade and Coke. He explains there is a single bottle of cider instead of cava for Pim, as he says she doesn't like champagne. He has bought a small jar of maraschino cherries for her as he supposes they have all tropical things like that in Thailand and I think it is touching that this small gesture is his way of saying welcome.

We arrive at the registry office in enough time to see Pim get out of Alf's son's car in a white tiered Cinderella dress. Pim looks so young she could be any age from about twelve to thirty. Alf appears from the pub opposite with gold ribbon tied around his walking stick. They do not adhere to the tradition of not seeing the bride before the wedding but walk in together. By the time we enter the main hall to the building there is already another crowd forming outside for the next ceremony which looks like it will be a young person's wedding. I think I recognise a couple of the women standing in their smart suits waiting, having a cigarette.

In the room where Pim and Alf are standing, him about a head taller than her even in her tiny doll heels, I am sat between Elsie, who is wiping her eyes with a hanky, a packet of boiled sweets in the dip in the dress between her legs, and Ruby, who has her hand in her handbag and is trying to pull back the tab from a packet of travel tissues. When she's got into them she nudges me and hands me two tissues, motioning for me to pass one on to Elsie. I stuff mine in my pocket.

There are ten of us including the couple to be. Alf has two old friends from the pub who haven't worn ties and are in casual V-necked golfing jumpers, they all have matching red noses and when they walk past I can smell they have been drinking. They usually come in the caff with him later in the afternoon with brandy on their breaths after the last horses have run their races. The remaining guests are two old ladies in hats with miniature veils, brooches and white gloves, who I find out later are Alf's religious twin sisters. They sit on the other side to us with his son, still keeping the formalities of a church wedding alive. Pim has no guests but later at the party she shows me a photograph she had folded in her bra and points to a large group of people eating melon at a table who I guess are her family.

During the ceremony, which is about five minutes longer than it would have been due to Pim having to repeat what the registrar says painfully slowly as her English is not so good, Pim giggles inappropriately when she says 'I do'. You can tell she has been rehearsing the other bits with Alf over and over again and I want to jump up and say the words for her. When she says Alf's name, she pronounces it as if she was barking like a miniature dog, saying 'Aff I take Aff', and he shakes his head and mouths the words while she is saying them, coaxing her along like a primary-school teacher.

He holds both of her hands throughout the service, which is touching, but when they are told they can kiss at the end we all look away, fidgeting in our chairs, finding other things to do, as it is slightly too sexual to be comfortable. He has his hand between her bottom cheeks, pressing the space hard and pulling her up towards him, making her stand on the points of her high heels as he pushes his tongue into her small mouth. Elsie blows her nose loudly and thankfully he lets go and Pim stands looking up at him and says, 'I love you, Mr Aff.' And we applaud as much for the clear pronunciation as for the sentiment. Alf looks proud, knowing he has taught her the correct phrases he wants to hear. They walk out of the room and we scrape back our chairs and follow.

Now we are outside in the sunshine, we all take it in turn to wish them happiness and Pim smiles, not knowing what we are saying. While the twin ladies come over and say hello, Alf has lit a cigar with his friends and we are discussing how lovely it is that the sun is shining and behind the twins Alf's son is giving Pim a long bear-hug, moving her silky straight hair, planting a sloppy kiss on her neck which I am not sure is entirely appropriate.

To the side of the entrance, we remain standing on the steps, emptying the last out of our confetti boxes into the air. Elsie has scattered some in our hair and has that childlike glint she sometimes gets in her eyes. Then there are the obligatory photographs which I take with Alf's son's camera. The twin sisters having lifted their tiny veils, the son and the happy couple squeeze into one tiny frame for a few shots and then we have a group one which we get someone from the next wedding group to take.

We are discussing how to get back to the caff, whether to get

the bus or a minicab, when out of the blue I see a familiar hairstyle and before I can prepare for it, I know who it is walking
towards me.

Sally. Sally is dressed in cream and lace and has small white
flowers in her pinned hair. She looks as if she is in a daze. Fat
Neck has a trendy suit on with a plump purple tie and a flower
in his buttonhole. I duck behind Ruby, but accidentally stick one
of my chopsticks from my hair into her back and she yelps. Sally's
eyes flit towards me and her face sinks after she has quickly looked
me up and down. Ruby can only hide half of me. Sally then steps
behind Fat Neck and I can see she must be talking to him about
me because he turns around angrily and starts to come over but
she is pulling at his arm to try to make him stop.

'Why don't you just leave us alone, you freak?' he shouts and
Ruby thinks he is talking to her because I can see she has taken
in a deep breath and lifted her chest and head. My stomach sinks
and Alf's son comes over to see what the commotion is.

'Who are you calling a freak, boggly eyes?' Ruby shouts, pointing
back at him, and I remember how Ruby always sticks up for herself
and doesn't take any nonsense in the caff and how she says at her
age you should be able to look after yourself and not care what
people think.

Ruby's right, you know, I hadn't noticed before but Fat Neck's
eyes do bulge like a fish.

Sally pulls him back to face her and is clearly furious with him.
Her face is set with that look, the one she'd found for the end of
our relationship and I thought was unique. She storms into the
registry office and disappears into the ladies' toilets and Fat Neck
runs up the steps behind her, revealing his purple socks, and waits
outside knocking on the door and calling her name. And I feel
relieved that it's not me and it's his turn now, because that look
that she's just given Fat Neck is the same one she gave me the
day Fat Neck spooned erotic lasagne into her mouth, her birthday,
when I barged into the pub and said in a loud voice, 'What the

hell is going on?', all soap-opera style. The same hard flinty look she'd had in her eyes when she took me outside and spelt it out to me. And maybe, although Sally won't ever speak to me again, maybe that time is getting closer when she'll tell Fat Neck where to go and it'll all be over.

We leave them to it and our group disbands and Alf's son drives the couple in his car back to the caff and we follow behind with one of the twin sisters who had parked at a bus stop and amazingly not got a ticket. In the back of the car, sitting on a crochet blanket which covers the back seat, the twins in the front, one of them driving with her gloves on the padded wheel, Ruby links arms with me and says, 'You were far too good for her anyway, just remember that.' And I look at her amazed, as she'd never met Sally before and how did she know as I had never discussed it with her, and then she simply says, looking straight ahead, 'Elsie showed me, it was always in the tea.'

38

From standing on the shimmering wet pavement below my flat I can see that my bedroom light is on and there is a slow flickering of white light from the television on the woodchip wall, high above the sofa. The curtains are drawn in my bedroom and unless she stands up, I will not be able to know for certain if Kate is still in my house, but the signs are all there.

I have just left a conga along the street started by Alf's son and I am waiting for Petula to catch up as she is lagging behind, swaying dangerously towards a parked car. I haven't mentioned the letter and don't think I will unless she brings it up one day. The party was a success although we had to wet kitchen roll with cold water and put it on our lips from Ruby's Thai curry, it was so spicy.

A few hours earlier, as soon as Petula came through the door of the caff, I could tell something was wrong with her. She had come straight from work with her name badge still pulling at her blouse and before speaking to anyone had headed straight for the free wine, filling up a plastic cup to the top. After she had downed the wine, head back, like a marathon runner would a bottle of water, she'd come over to me and said looking at her feet that she'd lost her mobile phone or maybe had it stolen, she couldn't be sure. But she was bloody cross about it, as, along with the phone, had gone the saved treasured messages from Ivor and the bouncer. Messages, she'd said, kicking one shoe against the other like a teenager, which she'd kept so that when she was old and ugly she could remember how much she was fancied and how good she was at blow jobs.

But now in the street, below the light from my windows, as I turn round to look for Petula, I see she is bent over about to be sick down the side of a parked car, holding on to the wing mirror. I go and lift up her hair and rub her back and when she is finished hold her arm and direct her up the front path. I open the door and have to ignore what could be going on upstairs for now and unlock her door with my emergency key and she groans her way into the flat and pads onto the sofa.

'It's all lost. It's all over,' she says throwing herself face down on it. 'I never wrote their numbers down anywhere.' I get the blanket out of her cupboard and spread it over her.

'It'll be OK,' I say. 'You get a listed phone bill, remember. It'll have all the numbers on there.'

'I don't know what to do without it. I feel like something's gone forever and I don't know how to get it back.' She starts to sob into the cushion on the sofa.

'I know,' I say. 'We'll get you a new one. It'll be better than ever, I promise.' I go and get a bucket from under her sink and fill it full of hot water with a bit of washing-up liquid and go and throw it down the side of the car where she was sick. By the time I get back in Petula is asleep on the sofa, her mouth all misshapen on the cushion. As I think about the letter I bend over and kiss her gently on her forehead and her eyes flicker and she makes that mouth movement where you are eating nothing but the comfort someone gives you in your sleep.

I am upstairs outside my flat. Pausing, before I enter, I try to imagine what I will say to Kate, as I fear she must still be here in my bed or in my clothes on the sofa. I wipe the dust off the edge of my letter box and scratch at the residue of some old Sellotape which the pensioners before must have used on it once and then take a deep breath and go in. From the lounge there is the sound of a man reading the news. I walk past the bathroom and the light is on and there is milky used bathwater in the bath. I can still feel the steam and the smell of my bodywash in the air from it being so recent. Then a female newsreader's voice comes on and it's one of those special reports and I can hear she is talking about a family's disappointment at the verdict of a young nurse's murder inquiry.

The bedroom is empty and the bed is made so that it looks like the duvet has been stroked perfectly flat, like they have in the photographs of hotel rooms in Petula's brochures. It is all so neat and unlike anything I imagine a student to be capable of doing. There are fresh Hoover marks across the bedroom carpet like small connected Vs. I creep along the corridor to the lounge and almost daren't put my head round the corner. I see a rucksack with a pair of high heels balanced on top and several stuffed carrier bags full up to the handles and two long feet in tights on my rug, the line of the seam stretched perfectly over the end of the toes. The feet belong to legs which reach up to a brown woollen skirt and a cream woollen fitted jumper with two Marilyn Monroe pointy breasts underneath. And I see her surprised face, a beautiful familiar face of fine cheekbones with a dusting of rouge and shaped eyebrows overseeing black mascaraed eyelashes looking up at me and I can't believe it. Near to my left on the wall is the pinboard and I see the photo of Mum all ripped but joined together and I glance at the person on my sofa and back to the image and realise that she is, probably quite unwittingly, wearing the same coloured clothes as Mum did in that photo and the wig is not quite the same style, but it's practically a bob like hers was and is the identical auburn shade.

'Oh my God. How did you know where I lived?' I say.

And Amanda says, smiling, 'I've always known where you are, silly.'

'But how did you get in?' I say.

'A girl called Kate with a really bizarre hairstyle let me in earlier just as she was leaving. She left you a note on the side. Do you know her? Well, anyway . . .'

And she stops right there, then she gets up and I can see the lifting of one of her false eyelashes in the corner of her eye where it needs a little glue and I gently push it down, back into place, but it lifts again. She smiles, looking at me and puts her long strong arms around me and I can feel her breasts slightly higher than mine, the bumpy firm texture of bean bags, pushing into me, my face in her shoulder, keeping my heart from flying onto the carpet, and somewhere a camera flash goes off and it all stays still.

Just for that quick instant.

Acknowledgements

I'd like to thank the Chardonnay grape, which aided the many nights with my friends Angela, Ali, Emma, Kate, Lucy, Charlotte, Elaine and Karn, who listened to me read the work, trying to get it right. Gratitude to Northern Jo for her sandy retreat; Southern Jo and Abi for their sparkling insights; Sonia for her Brighton base; and Jane for her inimitable wit; Julia Darling for being around (even if not physically); Ali Smith for being Ali Smith; and Nicola, my agent, for all her invaluable support and enthusiasm; my family for their love; and Mum for keeping me real and reminding me not to 'burn the candle'. And lastly, a special thanks to Minnie, my yellow tulip, only you know how much you've helped.